A Long Walk

World of the Dead, Volume 1

Traverse Davies

Published by Bright Crow Publishing, 2019.

A LONG WALK

First edition. April 16, 2019.

ISBN: 978-1989584132

Written by Traverse Davies.

Get the sequel for free!

It's been twenty years since the dead rose to consume the living, and humanity has survived, at least in one small corner of the world. The city of New Hope is growing and running out of space so they send a force out to take back a nearby island from the hordes of zombies that shamble through its streets.

The island is home to another group of survivors though, a cannibal cult that worships the undead and doesn't want to share.

Chad is young, newly trained, he finds himself in the midst of hordes of zombies as the only member of his squad not captured by the cannibal cult. It is up to him to save the rest.

Tamra is an actress on the only TV station left on earth, but she wants to be more, she wants to be a real hero. She throws herself into the middle of the mission, heedless of her own safety. Skills she developed in the early days of the post-apocalyptic period.

Tyson worked construction, trying to reclaim resources from the ruined world. The cult captures him and now he must struggle every moment to survive and to maintain his sanity.

All of these disparate characters are desperate to return to their home, to survive, to defeat religious fanatics and thousands of undead who still wander the world.

You can get Resource Economies (book 2 of the world of the dead series) for free! Just subscribe to my mailing list [1]at http://bit.ly/2K99oBP-resource-economies-free-ebook and I will send it to you. I use my list to keep my readers up to date on what I'm doing and what I'm writing. I will never sell or give away your information.

---

1. http://bit.ly/2K99oBP-resource-economies-free-ebook

A Long Walk
Traverse Davies

A cknowledgements

Thanks to my son, Alex. He has always made me proud. I also owe a huge debt of Gratitude to Linda Bowes for editing support above and beyond. Thanks as well to Reddit user JelzooJim (http://jelzoo.com/) help with cover design, and to my cover model Rhena.

There are many others, my Mother for giving me a love of books. Also, the school system for giving me a desire to escape this world and be part of another one, any other one.

And finally, if you are reading this, thank you for deciding to pick up my book.

Meet Jasper

Jasper was running through the pre-dawn light, breath heavy and ragged, heart pounding in his chest. The street lamp up ahead left a pool of light on the ground; it looked like sanctuary, rescue, salvation. An illusion of course; one made stronger by the tunnel of vegetation that he was passing through, the darkness of the hot summer night. At his heels, his dog Snow was just hitting his stride. Jasper's headphones played an old track by Faithless that helped him keep his pace, toes striking pavement with every beat.

His mind wandered on his morning runs, a way to sort out his life, put everything in perspective. His divorce, not a recent pain but recent enough, the more recent pain of Karen taking Taylor to live in Charlottetown, the fact that he was burning out in his career. Not quite forty and already probably gone as far as he could, the fact that he hated his house, hated where he lived. The house was Karen's idea. It was in a good school district, but it looked exactly like all the other houses. The area was nice, but it took too long to get anywhere.

Still, when he ran, he could put it in perspective, the pain in his limbs reminding him that he was still human, that at his core he was an animal, a predator, that the world he had so much trouble adapting to wasn't the real world, just a pale reflection of it.

Snow startled at a shape in the shadows. The dog wasn't precisely a coward, but he was nervous of the dark. The shape resolved itself, another early morning jogger. Jasper gave a brief nod and kept going. The voice in Jasper's headphones informed him that he had reached the halfway point, two point five kilometres. He turned around and began the run back home.

Traffic was light as he made his way up to the Bedford Highway and then ran south towards his suburb. He thought about how much the area had changed. When he was a young man this was where the wealthy lived. An exclusive area where the police came faster than throughout the city, where people like him weren't welcome. He used to visit friends here, hassled by those same police for his poor clothing, white trash not appreciated. Back then you rarely saw any non-white faces in Bedford, and his group of friends was mixed race which made them even more of a target. Now it was one of the more diverse areas of the city, boasting a significant Arab population for starters.

He kept a good pace as he ran up the hill to his street. The house loomed, feeling like a trap. Karen wanted to be in a safe area, to give their daughter every chance for a decent start, and Jasper went along. Moving in when Taylor was only five. Eight years later the place was too large for just him and Snow, but he was having trouble getting it to sell. Meanwhile, he felt like a stranger there, because with the threat of having to show the place it was staged to look neutral, devoid of personality. Everything that made it his was hidden or in a storage locker. He went inside and took off his headphones. A quick shower, a smoothie, a cup of coffee, and a couple of caffeine pills and he was ready for work. The thought of going to the office filled him with an existential dread. Sitting there, writing code that he didn't give a damn about, trying to make small talk with a bunch of people who were every bit as disenfranchised and tired as he was, it was too much. He went outside and started his car; the oversized engine roared to life.

The car was his big indulgence. An impractical vehicle if such a thing had ever existed. It was something Karen would never have tolerated, which may have been why he bought it. A right-hand drive 1990 Nissan 300 ZX. It was fast, crazy fast. Terrible on gas, way too low to the ground for practical considerations. He was trying to figure out how he was going to get through the winter with it. He'd bought it after the snow stopped, after Karen left the province with Taylor, bought it really on a whim. The problem was he bought it without really thinking it through, and he didn't have enough money left over to get something practical. At least it made his one weekend a month trip to PEI more fun. Expensive as hell, but a fun drive.

Snow started barking from inside the house. This was unheard of. Snow had been his companion for three years and rarely barked. Jasper looked up from his phone and saw his neighbour, Mrs Tillman, heading towards him. She was wearing a nightgown, torn open, barely hanging off of one shoulder. Her neck was bleeding, and she looked like she was in shock... pale, moving with a slightly drunken gait. Mrs Tillman was in her mid-seventies and had been a widow for a decade already. Jasper helped her out around the house from time to time, and they often joked about how if it weren't for their partners they never would have lived there. She had moved into one of the first houses in the subdivision when it was brand new. She was funny, in an earthy sort of way, and not a stereotypical little old lady, but Jasper was pretty sure that she wouldn't usually be walking down the street with one breast hanging out of her flannel nightgown. She was quietly mouthing "Help me. Please way".

Jasper ran to her side, sprinting despite the pain in his legs from his morning run. She collapsed just as he reached her, falling into his arms. Slowly he lowered her to the ground. "Are you alright? Mrs Tillman? Abigail?". She didn't respond. Her neck wound was bleeding, a lot. Jasper knew from first aid training that people bled a lot more than what you see on TV, but this seemed to be a lot more than was safe. He pulled out his phone and dialled 911. He got a no circuits available tone. Something was seriously wrong - much more than an old woman bleeding in the street. His heartbeat sped up, the edges of fear setting in. What the hell was going on? He checked her pulse. It was there, faint, so very, very faint. "Mrs Tillman, stay with me. I got you. Just stay with me. I'm getting help." That was when he heard it. A low growling, animalistic, but somehow human at the same time. He looked towards Mrs Tillman's house and saw it, a child walking towards him, growling, head cocked at an impossible angle. It looked like the girl from two doors over, the far side of Mrs Tillman, Becky maybe? He thought Taylor had babysat her once. It couldn't be though, the way she was moving, stick like and stiff, shuffling. The child was covered in blood, the worst of it was around her mouth, running down her chin.

Jasper was a nerd, a huge one. His favourite show was The Walking Dead. He owned virtually every movie with "of the Dead" in the title. Half of his t-shirts had references to zombies on them. It still took him a minute to process. It's one thing to watch TV shows and movies about the dead coming back to life, and another to have an eight-year-old dead girl walking towards you on a quiet suburban street. That was what she was, of course, a zombie. Still, he got himself together well before she reached him and sprinted for his front door, leaving Mrs Tillman where she lay. Snow stopped barking as soon as he made it inside, satisfied that he had done his canine duty in warning his master. He stood ready, muscles tensed and waiting. Jasper slammed the door behind him, blocking the nightmare of a little girl walking his way. He shut out the chaos, took a minute to figure out his course of action. One thing was clear; he needed to get out of there.

Jasper had moved most of the survival gear into storage to make the place more acceptable to potential buyers, but he still had a few things hidden away in the house. It wasn't the full bug out bag that Karen had made so much fun of him for, but it was a start. His bow was first, a fifty-five pound recurve. A compound would have made more sense, but the recurve was what he had. Then he clipped the quiver to his belt. He considered leaving the bow behind; all his arrows had target heads on them, so they would be pretty limited but if he got a chance to get new arrows he would regret not having the bow that he had always trained with in his hands. Learning a new bow would take time, and he might not get any. He also strapped on the one real sword he had with him. A traditional European longsword, designed to be a hand and a half weapon. Finally, he grabbed his survival knife and put that on the other side of his belt, right next to his Leatherman. It wasn't much, but again, it was what he had. Usually, his bag would contain rations, potable water, all the essentials, but with the sale of the house pending his real estate agent had talked him into putting the survival rations in storage "just for a little while". She seemed to think it might be off putting to potential buyers.

He knew exactly where he was going. He had to make it to Charlottetown, to Taylor. He needed to find his little girl.

Finally, he grabbed Snow's leash and headed out the door, calling the big husky mix to follow him. Becky was still coming, walking her stiff, jerky way over to him. He knew that moment, the one in the movie where the zombie closes in and the hero recoils in shock and horror, aghast at what he has to do. Jasper wasn't a hero though, he was too practical for that. He had trained for survival and had been through enough as a teenager to act without hesitation. Instead, he pulled his sword and swung, not taking the time to think about what he was doing. The sword cleaved into her skull, splitting it. She dropped, whatever had been animating her suddenly gone. Apparently, the movies had gotten more than a few things right. He knew that later when he had a chance to process this would mess with his head, but in the moment, it was what he had to do, and nothing more. There were a couple more problems though. Mrs Tillman was getting up and more figures were shuffling down the hill towards them, moving in the same jerky was as Becky had.

Jasper opened the car door. Snow jumped in, taking up his customary spot in the tiny rear seat. Jasper sheathed his sword and tried to get in the vehicle, but the sword kept getting caught up. Finally, he pulled it back out and dropped in the passenger seat, the flexible sheath folding up out of his way.

He slammed the powerful V6 engine into reverse, backing out of the driveway at nearly full speed, spinning as he went so he was facing down the hill. The ground clearance being what it was, the bottom of the car scraped the road, throwing up a shower of sparks.

Jasper accelerated down the hill as fast as he could. It felt like being punched in the chest. An average car would never have been able to take the winding cul-de-sac at that speed, but the Z handled the turns without issue, staying glued to the pavement. He rounded the corner onto the Bedford Highway, and barely managed to avoid slamming into the large pickup truck that was stopped almost directly in front of him. He was trapped between the truck and the ocean, nowhere to go. "Fuck." Both directions were full of cars, stopped. That was normal in the morning; the Bedford Highway was a major artery, and at rush hour it got pretty bad. On this morning though figures were shambling through the traffic, grabbing at people who dared to leave their vehicles. The car wasn't going to work, not here, there was no way he could get through. "Come on Snow; we have to ditch. Let's move it, buddy." Talking to the dog was an ingrained habit, starting when Karen and Taylor moved out. He climbed out of the car quickly, grabbing his sword, and once again began to run. Snow followed, his long legs far fresher than his masters. He headed through the grocery store parking lot, trying to get to the boardwalk behind it. He sprinted, feet pounding the pavement, adrenaline making up for his tired, sore legs. There was a crowd already in front of the grocery store, trying to get in. Better to skip it, play it safe, get supplies when he had a chance.

There was a small gap in the fence behind the grocery store, low to the ground. Jasper slipped under it, to the nearly empty boardwalk and started running with his steady long distance stride. Five K, his typical morning run, wasn't nearly enough to get him out of the city, and he had already done it once today, but he needed to manage some distance. He knew he had to cover miles, get out of the crowds, find a place that was secure to hole up and recover his strength. His mind started ticking off a checklist. The rule of threes, three hours without shelter, three days without water, three weeks without food. The practical nature of the list kept him from focusing on the larger problem. At least the route was familiar; he was running almost the same way he ran every morning. He passed the high-end condos, some of which had groaning, shuffling zombies trying to get at him through the privacy fences that surrounded all of them. Here the undead were kept behind barriers for the most part. One of them was on the path ahead of him though, an older man, in good shape, wearing jogging gear. He was a regular; someone Jasper would nod to most mornings. Jasper didn't even slow, drawing his sword as he ran. He swung while ducking right around the man. His blade didn't hit solid, catching the creature's left arm, way off target. The shock of the steel biting bone almost wrenched the sword from his hand, but he held it, turning as he pulled the blade free. The creature reached out for him with its one remaining arm, so Jasper took that one too, cutting it off at the elbow with a single hard swing. Nothing but a dark ichor came from the wound, almost black. He threw a push kick into the creature's hip, sending it back a pace. As it approached again, he took its head off, putting his back and shoulders behind the blade. Thankful for all the hours spent practising swordplay he turned and ran on.

The path, earlier so dark and threatening with its rows of trees that almost met overhead was now a beacon of hope. Out of sight of any houses, it was unlikely to be populated this time of day. He kept pace though, knowing that there was a limit to what he could do, that eventually his legs would stop moving, and that he was close that point. He moved onto the deserted path and finally stopped running. Snow stayed close, a half pace behind him as always.

Shore Drive was just ahead. He had to move on, out of the safety of the wooded path, but Shore Drive was a winding street with lots of cover, easy to miss a zombie there. There weren't a lot of houses on the road, at that point only on the harbour side. Who knew how wide spread this was though? There could be hundreds of zombies just ahead of him. He wanted to steer clear of people for the moment, at least until he had a better grasp on the situation. It seemed like the undead were attracted to the living from what he had seen in the last few minutes, not to mention from countless TV shows and movies. The yellow house. It was perfect, was well kept up, but had been for sale for the last few years, and he was fairly sure it was empty. He crept, careful to stay out of sight of the road, right to the end of the path. Then he checked along the road to see if he could spot anyone. It looked clear, and the yellow house was just in sight. He needed to find a way into the house, to hole up for a little bit, at least until he had a chance to catch his breath. The place was set back from the road and secluded, empty. He sprinted for all he was worth, almost at the end of his energy and hit hill next to the driveway, sliding down it. The house was huge up close, even larger than he thought it had been from a distance. He ran around to the back door and tried the knob. It was locked, of course.

He checked one last time, made sure Snow was with him, then slammed his heel into the door right next to the lock. He heard the splintering sound of the frame giving way, one more kick and he was inside. There was an alarm panel on the wall, beeping in anticipation of the correct code. He grabbed it and pulled it out of the wall, tearing all the wires out. The panel went dead and with it the alarm. He took a moment to look around, breath ragged and hard. This room was hot pink, modern, jarring in its normalcy. In his head, it should have looked derelict, on the edge of ruin. He knew that was irrational, that whatever was going on had just started in the last few minutes, of course, the house was still fine. There was a wood stove, a treadmill, and some nice leather furniture, but he thought that his realtor would be horrified by it. No wonder the place hadn't sold. He muscled the treadmill over to block the door, leaving it more or less secure. It would have to do for now. He made his way further into the house, up the stairs to the main level, keeping his body flat against the wall, taking the corner fast, moving into the room at unexpected angles. When the room turned out to be empty, he felt foolish for a moment, like a child playing at being a spy. The walls transformed from the hideous pink to an equally terrible hospital green. The ceilings were about thirty feet high, with floor to ceiling windows on the back wall, filling the room with light. The view across the harbour was unreal, letting him see the city proper.

There was smoke everywhere. It looked like half of Halifax was on fire. How had it started so fast? Minutes, just minutes and things were already falling apart.

First, water. All the running had left his mouth parched. He tried the taps in the kitchen. The water was still flowing, as he expected. The area was on a gravity flow system, water usually worked even when power failed. The water was cold and clean. He sipped at it, slowly. He counted each breath, four in, four out, until his breathing calmed down. What the fuck had just happened? Had he just sliced through a little girl and an old man? Zombies. He started shaking, his muscles cramping and seizing from the adrenaline dump. His eyelids were lead weight, dragging, closing on their own, the room was starting to spin, his head felt like it was going to lift off his shoulders.

Upstairs, to the bedrooms. He fell prone onto one of the beds, and Snow jumped up next to him, loyal to a fault trusting his human to know the right thing to do. Sleep was instant. Jasper dozed on and off for the next few hours, sporadically wakened by distant sounds of sirens, gunfire, explosions, screams. By the time he woke fully the sun was setting, casting long shadows across the room. Time to get going. Taylor was waiting for him (had to be waiting for him, the alternative wasn't something he could think about).

The evening was warm, smoke thick in the air, making breathing hard. The sun was low on the horizon providing shadow to move through. Jasper crept, his legs bent, body low to the ground, at this point speed had to take a back seat to stealth. He kept one hand on the hilt of his sword as much as he could, to keep it from tangling in his legs more than to have it ready.

There was a yacht club on Shore Drive, a small one with a half dozen boats in. Part of him wanted to grab one of the boats and set sail, avoid all the risks of going overland, Charlottetown was also a port city. Of course, he didn't know anything about sailing, so he kept moving past the small building and all the boats with a sigh of regret.

His muscles wanted to run, his hunched posture putting more strain on his legs than just letting his stride take him, moving as fast as he could away from there. It was so tempting, but around him there were shambling dead people, walking slowly, aimlessly. He was sure he could handle one or two easily and with the right position even four or five. There were dozens even on this sleepy side street. If they realised he was there, he would stand no chance. One of them got close to him, so he lay down, staying as still as he could. He started to feel cold despite the warmth of the evening, the ground, at first pleasantly cool, was sapping the heat from his muscles. His stomach felt hollow, empty. The thing moved away, shuffling down the road. Time to get up and keep going, agonising step by agonising step. Full dark had set in, and even with the fires, it was hard to see anything.

Out of the blue Snow let out a snarl, quiet enough that it didn't carry, and then there was a thumping sound. In the half light, he could make out the white dog sitting on the chest of a zombie, an older man with a large gut. The man was trying to bite Snow, jaws snapping, neck at an angle that he could never have achieved while alive. The big husky mix held him down, a paw on either shoulder. Jasper pulled his knife from his belt, pushed the creature's forehead to the side and slammed his thick blade through its temple. The creature stopped trying to bite, lying still on the ground. "Thanks, buddy," Jasper said, his voice no more than a whisper. He started moving down the road, a bit shaken, but also confident that Snow had his back.

Finally, a flash of light from a nearby explosion told him he had reached the small bridge at the end of the road; he had made it a full five kilometres from his house, a less than twenty-minute run achieved in a day

He moved quickly across the bridge, no cover to be had there, and into the small park right past it. Night had been a mistake. The zombies didn't seem to care about the darkness, while it crippled him. Better to move through as much of the day as he could, maybe just stay out of sight of heavily trafficked routes, stay off roads, be more careful. There was a small hut inside the park; door padlocked shut. Jasper used the hilt of his sword to break the lock as quietly as he could. With all the noise going on around him he risked being heard, even if it was a small risk as quiet as he was being, reasoning it was less of a risk than trying to keep going outside. Snow followed him into the hut, padding along on silent paws. He pulled the door behind him, and then took out his phone. The light from the flashlight app was almost blinding after the hours of moving in near total darkness.

The hut was, as he had always assumed, a storage shed for groundskeeping equipment. He decided to scavenge a bit, and then try to catch some rest. Despite having slept most of the day he was exhausted. Probably a combination of stress and lack of food he figured, so he did a quick survey of the room and then moved tools and random stuff into a pile, so he had a bit of clear floor to lie on. He put down some canvas sacks filled with soil and lay down on them.

A very bad morning

Robert was lying in bed. It was rare that he got to sleep in, but he had just come back from active duty and had a bit of R&R coming to him. Something brought him to consciousness, a movement in the bed next to him. He opened his eyes and saw his wife, Samantha. Something wasn't right about her, very far from right. Her mouth was open too wide, and her eyes were grey and dead. She was trying to bite him. Not a playful, sexy bite. No, she was trying to take a chunk out of him. He grabbed her by the throat careful to force her chin up so she couldn't get her teeth engaged and then lifted her slight frame with his powerful arms and threw her out of the bed. She crashed through the chair she kept at the vanity, reducing the mostly ornamental piece to splinters. His mind ticked through possibilities, what was happening. In a moment he knew what was going on. Hell, there was enough media out there to remove any doubt. Somehow Samantha was clearly a zombie. He decided that he needed to test it though, to define the problem space empirically. She was up and snarling, her arm at an impossible angle as a result of the fall, bone poking through the skin, but no blood just a small trace of a thick, black substance. He jumped out of bed, wearing nothing but his boxers. Samantha was five foot two, while Robert was six foot three. She was slight if toned; he was large and heavily muscled. He kicked the thing that used to be his wife and she went down, not unconscious or even dazed, just knocked off her feet. He dropped to one knee on its chest and grabbed a broken chair leg. He slammed it into Samantha's chest, breaking through her ribcage like it was nothing. She didn't stop trying to bite him. Okay, point proved, she was clearly a zombie. He pulled the jagged piece of wood out and drove it through her eye. Then she did stop like he had flipped a switch.

He got up, went to the wall safe and took out his forty-four rhino. A large gun, really too large for this situation. It was better suited to stopping large animals, but he liked it for the intimidation factor.

He was calm. Heart rate slightly elevated from physical exertion. He loaded the gun and then set it on the dresser next to him as he got dressed. He decided to wear his fatigues; they seemed like the most practical choice.

If Sam had turned in her sleep why hadn't he? Also, what about Robert Junior and Kayla, his children? He listened and realised he could hear a rhythmic thumping coming from the kids part of the house. So, probably zombies as well. "Okay. So, how do I deal with this? I have to make sure the children aren't a threat. Fuck. I'm talking to myself now." His ability to be rational surprised him. Robert had always known there was something wrong with him. An empty cold place in the core of his being that nothing seemed to touch. He thought about his children having turned, having to cave in their small skulls, pierce their brains, and discovered that he felt nothing. It was just a job that needed doing. Nobody had ever noticed, ever called him on it. He remembered once, when he was a teenager, he's tortured a fellow student, subtly driven him to the point of quitting school. The kid was a nerd, carried a briefcase to class in grade eight, dressed in suits. Robert had threatened to lock him in his own locker every day. He hadn't done it, but he was way bigger than the kid, could have done it easily. Never actually said anything overtly cruel to him, and was often friendly to him in public. Every morning "I'm going to lock you in your locker. You won't be able to get out." The kid was claustrophobic. Eventually, he had a breakdown, left the school and never came back. When he talked about why he left, he said it was because of Robert. When Robert's teachers asked him about it, he said he didn't understand "He's my friend, I have no idea what he thinks I've done." Robert had no idea what the kid's name was.

He laced up his boots, kept despite Sam's objections in the master bedroom, and got his kit together. A full pack, ready to go at a moment's notice. Enough gear to take him through a week or two on the road. Once he was fully equipped, including his pack and weapons belt, he headed out into the hall. The thumping was coming from Kayla's room.

He took out his bush knife. Zombies would require a quiet approach, and conserving bullets would be necessary. He opened the door. His daughter had turned as well. The pink room was a shambles, everything not attached to the walls knocked down. Kayla was wearing her footie pyjamas, pink with bunnies on them. Her curly blonde hair was dishevelled, in a way that Samantha didn't allow after she was up and dressed. Her eyes showed the truth. The iris was a washed-out grey, pupil missing. Her tiny jaw was opening and closing, with some sort of horrible internal rhythm, as if she was trying to chew the air. She came out moving as fast as her dead body would allow, grabbing for her father's leg, that horrible mouth questing for flesh. Robert swung the large bush knife straight down into her skull. There was a crunch and the knife sunk in several inches. Her little body went limp and fell to the floor.

Robert was pretty sure he should be feeling something, but nothing, just nothing.

Well, only one room left. Just his son. He drew his knife and headed for the door.

Fire and Water

Naomi was getting ready for work. Her roommate was still in bed, so Naomi tried to be as quiet as possible, not worth the hassle if she woke the bitch. The restaurant where she worked didn't have AC. It wasn't much of a restaurant, just a counter, a kitchen, and a couple of stools by the window. Most of the business they did was catering or takeout, but the food was made from scratch and tasty. The thing was, it was going to be hot out and with the stove running all day the place was always worse than the outdoors. She pulled on a crop top and a tiny pair of jean shorts, barely enough coverage to be considered clothes, the outfit left most of her smooth dark brown skin exposed. A lot of the customers stared at her, but the tips were way better days she dressed like this. For shoes, she grabbed her favourite strappy high heeled sandals. Work was at least an hour away by bus. Part of the joy of being broke. She lived where she could afford to, not where she wanted to. She'd been at the restaurant for two years, but only full time since she graduated high school last June, a single summer working for her aunt. It paid well, and it got her something to put on her resume, real work experience she could point to. She had a plan to get the hell out of this town, leave behind the ignorance, the poverty, the racism. The largest city in the province and still it was full of people with no ambition, people who saw as far as the horizon and no further.

Darryl was in the living room. Naomi didn't hate her roommate just because of Darryl, but he was a factor. Having her boyfriend sleep over every day, never paying rent, eating the food Naomi brought home from work. Naomi wasn't even sure Darryl had his own place anymore. God knew he never left. Berta was an issue all on her own, sleeping all day, dealing out of their apartment, but at least Naomi didn't have to put up with the same kind of crap from her.

"Hey girl, looking hot. When we gonna hook up?"

"Never. Get a job."

"Fuck you bitch. You know you want my dick."

"I wouldn't touch your skinny white dick if it was the last dick in the fucking world. Pay some fucking rent. Get a fucking job. Get the fuck out of my apartment. Oh, and stop eating my fucking food. Bitch."

Most of the time it seemed like he thought they were joking around with each other. Naomi wanted to stab him in his sleep.

She stepped out into the hallway, slamming the door behind her. The elevator was slow, and while she was waiting, Darryl came out, stood next to her by the elevator door. Was he actually leaving the apartment? A miracle. "What, you decide to look for a job today?"

"Got a court date."

"For fuck's sake. You know you gotta dress right for that shit right? Baggy jeans and a wife beater? The fuck you thinking?"

"Yeah, ho. Like you know shit. Those shorts don't even cover your skanky ass. Looks like you're working a street corner dressed like that."

"Yeah, well, I have a job. What you got? Why I bother trying to help your sorry ass anyway. I don't fucking know."

Finally, the elevator doors opened. Was that blood on the floor again? She hated living there, hated being poor, hated Darryl and Berta for being everything that everyone thought they would be and nothing more.

They stepped into the elevator together. Naomi was pretty sure Darryl hadn't bothered to shower. "What's the court date for? You knock over a convenience store or some shit?"

"Custody hearing. Trying to get my kids back."

"They'd be better off if you didn't. You know that right?"

"Fuck you bitch. What's a nigger cunt like you know anyway?"

"I should fucking stab your ass for that shit. Ain't your bitch a nigger too?"

"Yeah, I like dark meat. Don't mean shit though. Good enough to fuck, not for much else."

"Jesus Christ, the fucks wrong with you?"

Finally, the elevator hit the ground floor. Naomi almost ran out; she wanted away from Darryl, his ignorance and blatant racism. That's when the chaos hit her. Her apartment was on the ninth floor, and the windows were never open because even with the heat it wasn't worth it to hear the neighbourhood outside, the sounds of poverty filtering through the air. As soon as she could see outside, it was evident that something was wrong, very, very wrong. There was fire billowing past the building, and people were running, some screaming. She went to the door to get a better look, see if she could see what was causing the problem, Darryl crowding behind her, putting his hand on her ass, pig.

There was a car on fire just past the door, and crowds of people were surging around it. She saw one of them catch fire and fall to the ground. The crowd trampled him, nobody even pausing to help him up. Then there were others, slower moving, quieter, more deliberate. Every once in a while one of them would catch up to one of the running ones, usually when they fell. The slow ones started eating the fast ones every time they caught them. Even though there were a lot of people running the shambling ones outnumbered them by a large margin. The chaos in the street looked like it was going to spill into the lobby any moment, so she started towards her apartment. The elevator had headed up but was on the way back down. Darryl followed her, quiet now, his already pale skin even whiter. The elevator dinged and the doors opened. Two people were standing in the elevator, and another person lying on the floor, throat ripped out. The two standing had blood covering them, flesh hanging from one of their mouths. They turned, reached out, grabbing Darryl. He tried to pull away, but despite their slow movement, he couldn't break their grip. They pulled him down, as he screamed, sinking teeth into his flesh, tearing at him. His screams choked off with a wet gasp. Naomi ran for the stairs.

Naomi made it up a couple of flights when she saw movement coming her way, the jerking movement letting her know it wasn't anyone living. She ran down and headed for the first door she was able to reach, slamming it behind her. Her mind ticked off options, narrowing the list as circumstances became apparent. Limited options, but there were still a few viable ones, ways to get out of there.

She kept going until she hit the basement. Thanks to an ex-boyfriend who was obsessed with urban exploration she had been through most of the steam tunnels in the area, kilometres of narrow passages, some so small she needed to crawl to make it through, some large enough to walk upright. Don had been a huge nerd, not the kind of guy she usually dated, but the one she actually liked the most. He hadn't realised it, but she had loved exploring the tunnels. It was something nobody knew; she loved maps, navigation. Had since she was a small child, just another secret she hid from the world, another thing that got lost on her friends and family, they all saw the surface. She'd reached the point where she could navigate the tunnels blindfolded, escaping from her life down there, pushing herself to go further, learn more, instead of sitting in her apartment growing ever more resentful of her circumstances and her room mate.

As she was about to duck into tunnels, she spotted the janitor's work station. There was a pair of Chuck Taylors that looked like they were only a bit too large for her. She ditched the pretty sandals and threw on the sneakers. Sure, she would probably get blisters, but that was going to happen either way, and her odds of being able to walk were better if she wasn't wearing high heels. Sometimes pretty shoes had to take a back seat to practicality.

Entering the steam tunnels, she headed north. Any other direction just brought her deeper into the city. She didn't know how widespread this was, but it seemed like a good idea to get as far away from population centres as possible.

There was an exit that led into a small park, time to head back into the world. She had her backpack with her, a tiny one that was essentially a purse. She had her phone in it, but she didn't even know who to call. It was clearly zombies, just like in the movies, and she had no family she cared about. Her aunt wasn't someone she liked. Maybe she should call Berta, her roommate, but she hated the lazy bitch enough to be in favour of the zombies eating her. Instead, she started walking, checking for any movement.

She made it to the edge of the park before the zombies became an issue again. There were dozens of them on the street, wandering back and forth. It was a terrifying sight, most of them looked mostly ordinary, like people walking down the street, except they didn't walk right, shuffling and limping, limbs too stiff or too loose, heads at strange angles. A few were worse, burned, trampled, some bitten, all broken, horrible to behold. She wanted to scream, to run away, to curl up in a ball and die. Instead, she took a deep breath and said, "Okay Naomi. You can do this, just tramp it down. Deal with your emotions later, deal with this now," silently in her head.

The biggest question in her mind was where to go. The city wasn't safe, not even close, but she didn't have the resources or skills to live in the middle of the woods by herself. The airport was north, no people living there. Things had gone off the rails sometime late last night or early morning, so probably not that many people present. It was also very self-contained, with restaurants, a hotel, all sorts of things she could use. It wasn't far, but first, she had to get across the street.

A bad ending

Mona was running. The smell of burning was strong in the air. Fuck. Her trailer was on fire. Fuck. She'd set her trailer on fire. Fuck. Terry was dead. Fuck. She'd killed him. Set him on fire with the trailer. Fucker had tried to eat her. Fuck.

She kept running. A girl reached out for her. Mona smashed her as hard as she could. The girl went down, hard. Mona kept running. More, a crowd of them. She turned and ran another way. She was still high as fuck.

There was a house with the front door open. She ran inside, slammed the door as she went. One of them was inside. There was a fireplace. She grabbed the poker and smashed him in the head. Alive he had been a big guy. Still wearing his baseball hat and a loose fitting pair of jeans, no shirt. His rolls of fat spilt over the waist, a disgusting pale wave of dead flesh. She swung the heavy poker down, again and again, until the top of his head caved in. Then she ran out the back. Fuck. She needed a place, somewhere she could go and think. Needed to make sense of this. What. The. Fuck.

The school. She could go to the school. It would be safe there. Heavy doors. It was summer. Nobody inside.

She kept running.

Crossing the river

Morning broke early, filling the shed with filtered light, dust motes sparkling in the beams. Jasper was better able to see his surroundings, to take stock of what he had available. Once he realised how much light the shed let in he was horrified, he had been using his flashlight for an extended period the night before. A scratching sound at the shed door penetrated his mind. If it was only one zombie, he didn't think it would be a problem. Just slam the door open, and take off its head. If there was more than one, a very different story. He decided to gear up first, just in case he was wading into a group of the undead.

He found a tool belt, a compromise until he could locate a decent sized backpack, and grabbed some essentials. A medium sized pry bar was the best of it. It was going to be a pain in the ass to carry, but it would make getting into buildings much easier. It seemed like breaking and entering was going to make up a large part of his life for the foreseeable future.

Once he had a basic tool kit set up in the tool belt he drew his sword and made sure it was well clear of his belt, then he kicked the door, driving all of his weight into his heel. The door flew open, as the zombie that had been pushing on it fell to the ground. It was just one, so he decapitated it. The first swing didn't quite do it, the sword biting halfway through the creatures neck. A second swing did the trick. Snow followed, a moment behind him.

He had to cross the Bedford highway again in a moment, in order to make it into a path that would keep him off of the main roads, and for the most part out of sight. There were two paths he could take, the road crossed a small bridge, and there was a foot path that led under it, crossing a small river. It was hidden, would mean he could get across the road safely, but it popped up right next to the road, with no cover. He could be walking into anything, there could be hundreds of zombies right there, and he wouldn't know until they were on top of him. The other path was over the road, exposed the whole time. If he took that one, he would be able to see what was coming, to plan.

It was worth the risk after his experience the night before. He didn't want to be caught unawares again; Snow might not be able to save him this time. He crept up the embankment to a parking lot next to the road, surveying the scene ahead while staying as close to the ground as possible. His weight was on his elbows and toes, moving with almost a slither, belly centimetres from the ground. The strain on his shoulders was intense, keeping his weight that spread out, and he moved slowly, inch by agonising inch until he was in a position where he could see everything. His position was a bit above the highway, looking down at the chaos below.

The highway was covered in cars, empty of living inhabitants. The dead wandered between the abandoned vehicles, no pattern to their movement, no apparent logic to them at all. A grotesque tableau of decayed flesh. Even the intact ones had a quality to them, not just their too stiff movement, not just their grey and empty eyes, a slackness to their flesh, which made them horrifying. Jasper couldn't tell how many of them there were; hundreds at least, maybe thousands. They were spaced out though, not clustered. The stopped cars provided cover.

Slowly, moving in a crouch so his silhouette wouldn't be highlighted, Jasper made his way to the road. Snow stayed close by, eyes darting left and right, sniffing the air. The two of them crept up the stairs until they hit the sidewalk and crawled behind a van. So far so good, no increase in shuffling towards them. Jasper moved between cars, carefully and deliberately. He was almost across the street when his pry bar hit the side of a car, hard. The clanging sound spread through the street, and suddenly all the zombies were turning his way. Jasper leapt up started running. He hit a side street picking up speed, not even looking back. He could hear Snow panting next to him.

There was an office building not too far ahead, so he aimed for it, sprinting as hard as he could. The sprint was enough to give him a tiny bit of distance, get him ahead of the horde. Once he had some breathing room he slowed to a steady jog, settling into his long distance stride. He was still faster than the undead, and it meant he wasn't going to run out of steam too quickly, running down the side street until the building was in sight. It was new construction, large glass doors barring his way in. He jammed the pry bar into the gap between the door and frame and pushed as hard as he could. The door popped open with a loud squeal, the frame bent out of shape around the lock, glass still intact. He was developing a love/hate relationship with the pry bar. Jasper had never been inside this building before, but he was counting on it being like most small office buildings. Sure enough, there was a stairwell right inside the door, on the right. He opened the heavy duty fire door to the stairs and headed up, Snow on his heels. The zombies were catching up to him, his pause to open the main door had cost him time. He was counting on that. The zombies started milling into the building lobby, scratching at the stairwell door, trying to get at him, their weight pressed into it. Jasper ran up the stairs with Snow. If he had guessed wrong about the layout of the building he had no plan, no idea what he would do, everything depended on this one guess. He slammed the second-floor door open, headed for the back of the building. Once he got there he let out a breath he hadn't realized he'd been holding. There was another stairwell with the words "fire door, do not open" on it. Exactly as he had been counting on. He vaulted down the back stairwell hitting the latch on the rear door with an outstretched arm, and kept running. The tree line was right behind the building. He stopped running, wanting to make as little noise as possible, and moved slowly towards it. Snow seemed to pick up the need for quiet once again, slinking along next to him.

Finally, he was under decent cover. It was a small green belt, the kind you find in suburban neighbourhoods to make them feel more like you aren't in the city. He moved slowly through the trees and back to the street, around a bend and out of view of the office building.

The highway continued on the other side of the river, a natural barrier between him and the zombies that hadn't chased him. The ones that had were long out of sight, not following any further.

He made his way down to the path next to the grocery store parking lot. He was hungry, hungrier than he had been in years, it felt like his stomach was eating itself. The last time he was that hungry he was doing his survival certs in mid winter. Snow would be at least as hungry as he was. The grocery store was tempting, incredibly tempting. He crept along the path with Snow, keeping low to the ground. He rounded the bend so he could see the front of the store. It looked safe, no zombies clustered out front, no people trying to break in. A lot of blood near the doors though, clear indication that something went down yesterday. A bad sign: the door was wide open, and the lights were out. There were better stores in the other mall across the highway, but no way was he trying that crossing again.

He moved through the parking lot, scanning from side to side, head up. He made it to the front door, it was jammed in place, random bits of trash blocking it. Inside he could see that the second set of sliding doors were closed, the lobby trashed. No food in between the sets of doors. Jasper moved to the inner doors, pushed the pry bar in between them, leaning his weight on it, hard. He heard something moving inside, shuffling towards him. Three zombies shambled into view. It was a gamble, it was possible that the horde from the office building would still hear him, but he was so hungry. He decided to chance it, but cautiously, methodically. He pushed the doors most of the way shut, leaving a thin gap between them. He pulled one of the large tables over to the outside doors and upended it so it was blocking the entryway, making as little noise as he could. The noise he did make was enough to pull all the zombies he could see right to the door. There were more than he had thought, ten or twelve it looked like, all clustered near the door, trying to push through. The door was starting to slide, so he drew his sword and stabbed the closest one through the head. The creature's skull provided resistance for a moment, so he pushed harder, until finally it smashed through the bone, right through the back of the head. Pulling the sword out was harder than he had thought it would be. Another one filled the gap as soon as the first one fell, teeth gnashing. An older woman, heavily made up. Her body was torn in a dozen places and her throat had a gaping wound. There was a strong smell of shit coming from her, and probably from all of them. He hadn't encountered them indoors before, and not in these numbers. The smell was worse than he had imagined. He knew that dead people would lose control of their bowels, but it hadn't occurred to Jasper that meant zombies too.

He slammed the blade forward again, catching her at a bit of an angle, so it sliced off a large hunk of her cheek and some of the flesh on her head, just surface damage. She didn't even flinch, continuing to try and bite him, teeth gnashing in the gap of the doors. He pulled the sword back again and slammed it forward on target this time. He realised the doors were starting to slide, and there was no way for him to brace them, he needed to pick up the pace and pick it up now. Desperate, he started slamming the sword into the undead as rapidly as he could. By the time the doors opened wide enough for them to spill through there was only four left. The first one fell to the floor as Jasper swung his blade. He caught the second in the neck, but his blade was coming at a downward angle. It bit into its far shoulder, lodging there and pulling out of his hand as the zombie fell. Snow jumped on the back of the one on the ground and started biting at the back of its neck, keeping it pinned, but that left two coming at him while he had no sword.

He backed up as he pulled the pry bar from his tool belt. The first one to reach him was a teenage girl, she might even have been pretty if all of her face had been there. Between the smell and the missing left half of her face she made him nauseous. Nothing in his life had prepared him for the smells and sights he was confronting.

On television it was sanitized, hidden behind glass. It was different when the rot, the decay, the excrement, was in his nose almost solid in its intensity. The wounds were wet, oozing, dripping. The zombies made noises too, not just moaning noises, wet squishy sounds as they moved, the sound of bodily fluids drying and pulling against flesh. He brought the pry bar down on her head as hard as he could, throwing all of his weight into the swing. There was a sickening crack, and she stumbled... but didn't drop. He drew back and slammed the bar down again. He knew that he had hit her with enough force to kill a human, but apparently it wasn't enough to actually destroy her brain. She was reaching for him with hands drawn into claws, he didn't have enough room to swing full force. The top of her head was deformed, bits of bone showing through her hair. He swung again, as best he could. Her fetid breath in his nose, blank dead eyes looking into his. The metal hit her already weakened skull, and finally she dropped. The other one was right next to her and got hold of Jaspers shirt, pulling itself towards him more than him towards it, before he had a chance to catch his breath. Jasper drove his weight behind the curved end of the pry bar and slammed it into the creature's mouth. This one was a teenage boy, long shaggy hair drenched in blood, left eye missing, right eye milky and empty. Jasper heard teeth crack and saw them fall out of the things mouth. He kept pushing, harder and harder. Finally he got some momentum and slammed the zombie back into the glass next to the door. He jammed his right shoulder against one end of the bar, and pulled his hunting knife out of its belt sheath. He pressed the blade against the zombies temple, while trying to hold it steady between his left arm and his right shoulder. Finally the blade started to sink in, eventually making it deep into its skull. The life finally went out of the creature and it dropped to the ground, just in time. Jasper had no strength left in his arms, his breath was coming ragged and hard, trying to draw enough oxygen into his lungs, an impossible task at that moment. That left just one. Snow had it immobilized on the ground, straddling its back. Jasper put both hands on the hilt of his sword and one foot on the back of the zombie and pulled the blade free. It wasn't too hard, with leverage on his side. The walked over, almost casually, and pressed the tip of the blade into the creature's head. He pressed down, then leaned his entire weight onto the hilt. The sword popped through the skull and the creature stopped struggling. As soon as it stopped Snow stopped fighting it, somehow knowing in his doggy brain that the threat was gone.

Now that he had a moment to breathe Jasper wanted to be out of there fast before the horde caught up to him. First, he hit produce and grabbed a bag of apples. Apples are portable and keep for a while even without refrigeration. He ate one on the spot, marvelling at how crisp it was, how good the juice felt bursting in his mouth, rain in a desert. After he ate and gathered his breath, he started scavenging. He headed for bottled water and grabbed a large bottle for Snow to drink. The big dog started lapping at it instantly, not even stopping when Jasper headed into the meat sections. Normally Snow got high-end pet food, but what could be higher end than top of the line t-bone steaks? It wasn't like they were going to be edible for much longer, and the dog needed to eat.

After Snow had his basic needs satisfied, Jasper started searching the store more seriously. He ate as he went, sucking up calories as fast as possible. He managed to find a medium backpack, a bargain brand leftover from last season that nobody had bothered with, not exactly suitable for his needs but better than nothing. There were a few other discounted items in seasonal meant for camping. He grabbed what he could, which was nothing much. There was one gem though, a few cans of alcohol gel meant for folding camp stoves. Just the dregs at the end of the season. There were also a few bottles of barbecue starter and a couple of barbecue lighters. He took all of that and improvised a sling for one of the four-litre bottles of water so that he could carry it around his shoulder. Finally, he had all he could carry, a bunch of tinned food, a can opener, a single can of pop, for the can, he still hadn't decided if he should drink it or empty it on the ground. He headed for the entry way. There were a few zombies in the parking lot now, but still not many. Jasper left by the fire exit, since it didn't have a giant table blocking it.

With a bit of food in his stomach things felt a lot more possible. Maybe he would be able to find a vehicle once he was out of the city and make his way by car most of the way. It would only take a few days that way. Karen was irritating, but competent. To be fair most people liked her, it was only Jasper that found her hard to deal with. There was something sticking in the back of his head though, something about the store. He put it aside to let his subconscious sort it out. One of the zombies spotted him right away, and started shuffling in his direction. He could see maybe a half dozen scattered around. There were bridges across the river leading to the parking lot he was in, and many, many undead on the other side of those bridges, he'd better be both quick and quiet getting out of sight. The path led along the river bank, and was far enough down that nobody from the road was going to be able to see him. Unfortunately that meant dealing with what was here fast. He drew his sword and moved on the approaching zombie. Fuck. Zombies. It hit him all of a sudden. He was swinging a sword at a zombie in the parking lot of the Bedford Superstore. This couldn't be real, not possible.

The moment passed as quick as it had hit him, he was too busy, had too much to accomplish. He took off the things head and kept moving fast. Two of the others noticed the movement and started to close, close enough that he didn't think he'd be able to lose them. The trail went under the first bridge, which meant he would have the advantage of cover and controlling the terrain if he could make it there before they could reach him. It would also mean that only one of them could get at him at a time. If they both tried they would end up in the river, which was swollen and overflowing its banks due to a wet summer. He half ran, half slid down the short slope by the riverbank and then moved fast into the hidden spot under the bridge. He saw one of the zombies come down, then another, then another, then another. Four. Shit. He'd managed to draw almost all the ones from the lot right to him. The first one came at him, a slow lurching crawl. He couldn't get a good swing at its head, so he aimed for its right leg, swinging as hard as his body would allow. He cleaved its leg from its body. The zombie fell into the water and was carried away from him. The river was high enough that even on the path he was up to his ankles, and the water was cold. He stood and waited. Snow was behind him, waiting. Suddenly he heard Snow leap, the water splashing, and a moment later saw the zombie that had been sneaking up behind him float away. The next three were easy. He only managed to dispatch one of them, but the river dealt with all four the same way. Even for a living person the current was intense. Apparently zombies weren't great swimmers. Nice to know.

Jasper kept to the path, but the path didn't go under the last two bridges, it ran up to them. He weighed the odds, but in the end, it was Snow that made him decide to go over on top of the bridges. The husky could swim, but he wasn't good at it, and Jasper wasn't about to risk the dog who had saved his life at least three times in the last twenty-four hours. He crept to the edge of the roadway, one hand on the dog's shoulder, keeping an eye for zombies. When Jasper couldn't see any, he popped up and sprinted across the road. He made the first bridge without attracting any notice. Jasper was even more cautious at the next bridge and managed it without problems. Finally, he was out of sight of the highway and could stay there for a long time.

The path Jasper and Snow followed passed through a green belt that lasted several kilometres and was almost entirely out of sight. The path led them past a chain link fence, crowded with a dozen or so zombies, all in military garb. The rifle range, Jasper had been hoping to check it out, see if he could get any weapons - did they even keep weapons in there? That was the one area Jasper had been nervous about, the path almost met up with a larger highway for a few feet before descending into tree cover. He passed between the broad road and the chain link fence on high alert. Too many zombies to check the gun range, all of them snarling and growling, trying to push through the distressed links. At least the highway was empty. He was in an area that was not really part of any area of the city, a transition between one suburb and another, not usually heavily trafficked in the early morning, probably never heavily trafficked again he realized. They moved onto the tree covered part of the path, crisscrossing the river as they went. The hard packed dirt under their feet made it easy to stay quiet, and the rushing river drowned other noises in its flowing depths. Jasper felt safer than he had since leaving the yellow house.

Around midday, Jasper stopped for some food. There was a small nook, with a bench and a shady view of the river, an idyllic spot he often stopped at when walking Snow. Jasper unpacked some crusty bread and sharp cheese, chased with bottled water, no longer cold but so refreshing. He poured a second bottle into a small dish for Snow. Despite the proximity of the river, Jasper was very, very careful with water supplies. He knew the Sackville River was heavily polluted, not potable drinking water, or even safe to swim in. The clear waters were an illusion. Maybe in a few decades, the water would be clear again, the damage done by his species fading.

Despite his fear, his need to make it to Taylor, the peace and tranquility of this spot seeped into him, calming him, letting his mind relax. If he was going to make it to Charlottetown he would need to plan, to think things through carefully. So far he'd been going on adrenaline and need, moving forward almost randomly. Every time he thought about Taylor he started to go into panic mode, what if she was alive right now, cornered somewhere, desperate for help? She was so far away, weeks at least if he couldn't get a working car. There was a voice in the back of his head telling him it was useless, but it was a voice he couldn't listen to. Every time it got too loud he thought about that moment in the hospital when he first took her tiny body in his arms, met her still closed eyes with his and introduced himself "Hi, I'm your father. I'm going to be spending a lot of time with you for the next few years." The smell of her, the warm softness, the feeling of life and potential from that new person, only in the world a few moments. She had nustled close to him, wiggling her little body so it made as much contact with him as possible, and fallen asleep. He just stared at her in wonder until the nurse came and took her away.

Finally, it clicked - the grocery store. Everyone in there was wearing a store uniform, and the inner doors were shut. How had they died? It didn't seem like any zombies had made it in from outside. This looked like a Romero situation, no way this had spread so fast if it was only transmitted by bite, more likely anybody who died got back up again. The store was different though. Why would somebody have died in there? No answers presented themselves. Jasper put it back on the back burner of his mind, something to worry about when he had the time. Break over; he started moving down the path again.

The rest of the day was spent traveling, and the one after that. He was still technically in the city, but in much less populated areas. Sleeping in hollows and relying on the weather to stay fair and warm. This area was full of single family homes, widely spaced, lots of green space to hide in. He saw zombies pretty frequently but for the most part he was able to stay clear of them. There was only one that spotted him from close enough to be a problem. He was crossing cul-de-sac when the zombie stumbled on him, stepping out from between two houses. It was the corpse of an older man, balding and wearing his bathrobe over fuzzy slippers. The tie on his bathrobe was loose, and the robe hung open, showing a distended belly, black with rot. The zombie started walking his way, shuffling with arms outstretched. Snow pounced, knocking him off balance. He tried to bite Snow, teeth gnashing. This time Snow wasn't able to knock him down, and Snow wasn't biting, even though his lips were pulled back into a snarl. Jasper pulled his sword, swinging at the old mans head. He was getting used to the shock in his arms, like nothing he'd experienced in training. Flesh parted, bone shattered, and the blade cleaved deep, burying itself through the skull, right into the old mans neck. He fell, lifeless and limp.

By evening of day four Jasper was exhausted and cold. He needed to find a place with shelter and security. Close to nightfall he spotted a school. It looked empty. The school yard was fenced in, although there were significant gaps for entry and exit points. He moved in, cautiously, sword at the ready. He thought heard something from inside, but when he stopped to listen, it didn't come again. Could be a zombie, but could just as easily have been a cat, or his imagination. If it was a zombie he would deal with it; he didn't see any other choice.

Robert at the Cottage

Robert was on the road. His goal was his hunting camp, a few hours out of town. Most of the route was on small back roads. He had abandoned his truck early, between the stopped cars and the zombies he had found it impossible. Every few minutes he needed to find a way to move something out of his way. Most of the time that would involve getting out of the truck and the sound of the truck drew zombies towards him. In the end, he'd had to lose half a dozen of the zombies that came up out of nowhere, which meant ditching the truck and moving forward on foot.

It was nothing new to him; he was used to long marches in full kit. Basic paid off once again. Now the camp was coming into sight. Some of the guys were clustered around, drinking, cooking food, making sure the place was secure. A good team; he'd been collecting them for years. Some people thought he was paranoid, building up this group, but in the end, he'd been right, and those people were probably dead. It had taken a very long time, finding guys he could trust, vetting them to make sure they were a fit for the team. Every time he was on a training exercise or active duty, he sought them out, quiet conversations about being prepared, about making sure the government wasn't taking too much from them, about property rights. His team, his guys. Loyal to each other more than country, more than unit.

A sound behind him made him turn. One of the guys, wearing civvies but carrying his service rifle dropped down on the path behind him. "Sir, glad you made it. We were starting to get worried."

"Thanks, son, it took a bit longer than I would have liked," Robert said, "Had to ditch my truck near home. How many made it so far?"

"We have twenty members right now, a few family members too. Total head count not including you is twenty-seven. Still hoping for a few more of course."

"Right. Your watch?"

"Yes, sir."

"Good work. I had no idea you were there. As you were."

The man drifted off into the woods, vanishing from sight almost instantly.

There was space for fifty at the camp, rough quarters, a small bunk for each man, not many amenities, but it was secure and hidden. Samantha had been upset about him using so much money for the camp, at least until he had a talking with her. The numbers surprised him; he hadn't expected nearly that many of his people to survive. The place was a hive of activity, preparations going on all around him. As the men started to see him many of them straightened up, throwing a quick salute his way, or just welcoming him. The fact was they weren't anything official, despite being almost all from a military background. He wasn't really a commanding officer either, just the guy who'd had the foresight to create this team, this place, to stock it at great personal expense.

"Gentlemen, glad to see so many of you made it," Robert said, "Looks like you are doing good work, making real progress. I have a few surprises for us, some things squirrelled away for a rainy day. I'll address the camp in an hour or so, in the meantime carry on with what you were doing." He continued into the main bunkhouse.

Originally this place had been a rehab centre, and when it went on the market, he snapped it up. Officially it was a hunting lodge now, used by Robert and his friends, occasionally rented out for large groups. There was a lot more to it than met the eye though. Part of why he had bought it was the cellar, not quite a bunker, but close. A large area under the main building with a heavy steel trap door, hidden under the floorboards. He had no idea why someone had built it, but there it was. He was one of two people who had a key, and it didn't look like Nick had shown up. Nick lived much, much closer, so he probably wasn't going to make it.

The cellar was packed, full of surplus gear, MRE's, tents, weapons, most of it bought under the table. Wouldn't do for the government to know exactly what he had. The weapons, in particular, were secret. He had half a dozen RPG's, tens of thousands of rounds of ammunition, a couple hundred rifles, all crated. It was enough to equip a small army, and that was what he had, more or less. Men had brought others with them. It was close to two hundred nation wide, most in Nova Scotia. A few were on active duty or stationed somewhere else. Too many were reservists.

"Hey, could some of you give me a hand?" Robert said. Two of the guys rushed over.

Robert handed them boxes. "I need to get all this stuff up to the main building, start doing an inventory."

They hauled boxes and crates for an hour. There was still a lot of it down there, but it was time for Robert to address the group. "Hey folks, so it looks like the world ended. Glad so many of you made it, and I'm still hoping for more. Anyone who started further out than me is probably still on route. Traffic's a bitch right now," This got a small laugh, "We have a lot to deal with right now. I prepared for almost any situation. I know we joked about zombies, but it was pretty much the only one I didn't take seriously. Well, shows how much I really knew. Anyway, it is what it is. I know all of us have lost people, but we're soldiers, we keep going. With that in mind, this is a good start point. I'd like to stay here as long as we can manage, but it's close to the city, it's not going to be viable forever. Eventually, the zombies will find us, and we will have to move. Could be a day, could be a year. We have to be ready for the idea that it's more like a day. Once we get the cellar unpacked we need to make sure we are able to move at a moments notice. For those who brought family: they are our number one priority. We protect the civilians, especially the children," Robert was getting the crowd going, getting them warmed up. They were eating out of his hand, "We will survive this, we, the prepared, the hard working, the self-reliant. The weak, the welfare leeches, the useless masses, they are part of the horde now, still trying to take a bite out of us. I say no more, this time we have the guns. We have the strength. This new world is ours for the taking!"

They cheered for him. Keeping it quiet, they weren't stupid, but as loud as they dared.

After the speech, Robert commandeered more of the men to help move stuff from the cellar. Inventory was going to take longer than he wanted to spend, they had to be ready to abandon this place at a moments notice. It was decently secured against most potential threats, but a horde of zombies was the one he hadn't taken seriously, so it wasn't set up for it. A scattered few buildings, too much space between them. No walls, no fences, they could be built but would need a large area. No cropland either. It wasn't farm country, too rocky; the soil was too acidic. An island would be better, someplace they could clear of zombies and then use. He called over Tom, currently acting as second in command. "Hey, I'm trying to figure out the best option for moving on from here. I've pretty much got it down to PEI or Cape Breton."

"Good points to both. Cape Breton's a bit closer. Too hilly though. We need space to grow stuff."

"That was my thinking too. A place we can build on. Plus, no rocks, right? Okay, that's the plan. Charlottetown area or Summerside?"

"Summerside. It's smaller, less zombies to deal with."

"Thanks, Tom, nice to have someone confirm my thinking."

The next few days were lost in prep. More people arrived, in the end, they had almost fifty including wives and children, although not many of those. On the morning of the day before they were ready to head out one of the scouts sounded an alarm. Robert jumped out of bed, dressing as he hit the ground. He ran out the door to find the source of the alert. One of the older men ran up, panting, "A horde sir, big."

"How big?"

"Too many to count sir. Coming right this way. Should hit us within the hour, even as slow as they are moving."

"Time to go. Pull the men back from watch, get armed."

Robert started waking the camp, moving fast, "Folks, get moving. We have less than an hour to be gone. Big horde coming. Wake up. Wake up!"

People started jumping out of their beds, wherever they happened to be. It took about fifteen minutes for the camp to be up and moving. Robert started triaging, getting the most essential gear loaded into backpacks and kits. Damn, he wished he could use a truck. It was close to the wire, and there was still equipment that needed to be loaded up, important stuff, but no time, the first zombies started to appear through the trees, and on the narrow dirt road. Just a trickle, the first drops in the flood. He brought his rifle to his shoulder and took out the lead zombies. Some of his men did the same. It might slow the horde for a moment. "Let's go!" Robert said, "Get moving now, leave whatever isn't already loaded!"

The camp as a whole started into the woods, following Robert. He looked back at the shelter he had spent so much time on as it was overrun, and then turned, moving forward.

No safety in the skies

Naomi spent the night in a dry culvert. It was uncomfortable and smelled of rot, but it was sheltered and hidden. When the sun came up, she started moving again. Her feet were covered in blisters; her legs were sore in a way she had never known. She was thin, but she was still young enough that it was natural, not the result of exercise. Her body wasn't used to sustained effort. Every inch of her hurt, every inch of her was exhausted. She was parched, she wished she had a bottle of water, and maybe some food. She was convinced she would kill someone for a bottle of water. There was water everywhere, on day one she'd taken a drink from a stream. The diarrhoea was unrelenting for the next two days. It had made her so much thirstier. Since then she's barely had anything. Out of desperation, she'd snuck into a convenience store, only to find it looted. She'd managed to find a bottle of some sort of sports drink, something that tasted like chemicals, warm. That was it for four days, and no calories. She was light headed and weak.

She had been moving from first light to nightfall for days. She was exhausted. The airport appeared through the trees, squat buildings deceptively tall, height masked by their breadth, dominating the landscape. She had pinned so much of her hope on reaching this place, and it wasn't going to work the way she wanted. The area in front of the main terminal building was a broiling mass of the undead, thousands of them. Apparently, on day one a lot of people had tried for this place.

Were there any other options open to her? She was closer to the runway than she was to the main building, and it was heavily fenced. Normally the fence would be a barrier she couldn't overcome, too many eyes, cameras everywhere, but now those cameras were blind, nothing but dead eyes to watch them even if the power needed to run them still existed. She moved to the fence stealthily. One stumble, but none of the zombies out front seemed to notice. The runway area looked like it was clear, nothing visible moving inside. She skirted the fence, moving away from the terminal. Finally, she found a spot. A tree was growing close to the fence, not right to it, but close enough. She climbed it, slowly, taking breaks. Then it was just a matter of shimmying out onto the closest branch, getting herself close enough, and hopefully not cutting herself on the concertina wire across the top of the fence.

First, she threw her bag over the fence, into the runway area, then she slowly started to move out onto the narrow branch. It was a fair ways above the fence, but it began to bend under her weight, bringing it close. Each inch pulled the branch down further and made it harder to hold onto until finally it touched the top of the fence and got lodged there. At last, a piece of luck going her way. She made it all the way across, never quite losing grip. Her head was spinning from the exertion. Naomi pulled the coiled wire on top of the fence out of her way, so, so carefully. She had it pulled out enough that she was able to get a leg up and over, then she slowly pulled the rest of her body across. The flash of pain was so intense she almost fell off, fifteen feet down to the hard packed ground, but she held it together. One of the wire coils had gotten away from her, and dug into her back, right along her shoulder blade. She took a deep breath and then slowed down even more. Finally agonising minutes later, her other leg was over, and she was climbing down. She had four or five new cuts, including the one in her shoulder. She dropped the last few feet down to the tarmac, almost falling when she hit the ground.

There were a couple of small buildings under construction inside the runway area, on the far side. There were also a few planes, but Naomi didn't know how to get to the doors and a couple of trucks. She started moving towards the buildings, eager to get out of the open when she noticed movement. They were still a ways off, but there were a few zombies in full ground crew gear. Thick helmets with earphones, orange vests, lurching slowly towards her. Nothing immediate, but far better to get out of the open, get into one of the buildings, preferably one of the ones with a door.

Naomi moved as fast as she could across the tarmac. She was tired and bloody, it slowed her down, but she was still faster than the zombies. She reached the buildings well before they did. One of them was just a shell, no features installed yet, window and door holes open, dark pits into the interior. The next was more of less complete, doors hung, windows in place. She tried the knob; it wasn't locked. The interior of the building was unfinished, drywall in place but not painted. The building was a single room, storage of some sort maybe, nothing but bags of cement and some old lengths of rebar inside. She shut the door behind her, turning the lock. The windows were small and high, light streaming in. There was a back door as well, she was grateful for that.

So, this was home for the moment. Time to get it stocked. One of the trucks on the tarmac looked like what Naomi thought food transport trucks looked like in an airport. She opened the front door, checked the progress of the dead ground crew. They were close, not right there yet, but too close for comfort, so she ducked out the back door. "Ha, I outsmarted you. Dead fucks," she muttered under her breath. The sound of a human voice, even her own, was a comfort now. She'd always liked solitude; now she was desperate for any human interaction.

Naomi was a ways from the building before the zombies noticed her, in fact almost to the truck. It had aluminium sides, diamond cut, on the rear section, and sliding panels that opened up. There was also a hatch on the back. First, she opened the sliding panels. The stench gagged her instantly. She almost threw up right there, the smell of rotten food filling her senses. There were rows of trays, pre-packaged aeroplane food ready for loading, all of it spoiled after days in the summer heat. She had to move though, search the truck faster. She opened the rear hatch. There was an open area, full of boxes. Bottled water, chips, snack packs of nuts, even miniature bottles of booze. Too much for one trip. She grabbed a bottle of water from the box and opened it, drank deep, then picked up a box of chip bags. Time to head back home.

Schools out for summer

Jasper tried the school door. It was locked. Maybe there was a better way in. Walking around the building, he spotted a fire door that was not quite completely latched. A zombie wouldn't be able to open it; you needed a tiny bit of brains, and some coordination, but not hard for a living human. Maybe there was somebody alive inside. Jasper hadn't seen a living person in far too long. He wanted to talk to someone other than Snow. The husky was a good listener but didn't give much back to the conversation. Jasper opened the door as quietly as he could, holding it open for Snow. The two of them checked the place room by room, methodically. Suddenly Snow took off down the hall, running full tilt, even barking a little, not his fierce bark, an excited almost puppyish sound. "Snow, wait, stop!" Jasper called, following a little slower, rounding a corner a little behind Snow. Snow was astride a ragged figure, pinning it to the ground. Jasper drew his sword and then creeping that the figure under Snow was laughing, that Snow was licking its face.

It was a woman, bone thin. She was dressed in layers of clothing, tied together with chord. Her laugh was quiet, high pitched and nervous. Jasper said, "Snow. Let her up."

The dog backed off, tail wagging. The woman stood, slowly but with a series of quick, twitchy movements. She wasn't that thin from just a few days without food, and the sores around her lips weren't new. Jasper had seen a few zombies that looked healthier. Still, she was alive. He said, "Hi. I'm Jasper, and apparently, Snow has already introduced himself."

"Mona." she spoke in a high voice that was too fast, words slightly slurred together, "I'm Mona."

"I have some food. It's not a lot, but I'm happy to share".

Her eyes lit up at the mention of food. Jasper looked around at the hallway, a nest of filth the woman had made for herself. There was an empty pipe made out of a lightbulb, an empty pot, a sleeping bag that looked as if it hadn't been washed in a decade, and a bunch of random detritus. Jasper was pretty sure this girl was a meth head, and that she was in the earliest stages of withdrawal. He set up his small camp stove, made from the empty pop can, and heated up a can of cream of mushroom soup. He gave Mona the last of the cheese and some crackers. She would be starving at this point, desperate for food. He was only a little hungry and figured that with it being late summer the cafeteria would have started to stock some things, so he could replenish his supplies pretty easily.

He didn't want to share dishes or utensils with Mona, he was afraid he would catch something, so after Jasper got her started eating, he told her that he was going to check out the school cafeteria to see if there was anything else he could use. She barely stopped eating to acknowledge he had spoken.

Jasper started looking for the cafeteria. After a couple of minutes, he found signs, and eventually managed to make sense of them. How did kids not consistently get lost in school? After wandering for a few minutes, he found it, a large cafeteria area with a kitchen in the back. The shelves were well stocked with large cans, and there was a walk in freezer, not to mention utensils and dishes. He would have to do something about carrying food though, his backpack wasn't nearly large enough. Hopefully, Mona could be convinced to come with him, well, maybe, hopefully. He hadn't decided if travelling with her was a good idea, but she was another person, and he needed another person - even if they would have to stay put for a couple of days while she went all the way through withdrawal. Best of all, the stove was gas which meant he would be able to cook while they were there.

He headed back to find Snow curled up next to Mona. The big dog opened one eye watchfully. Snow had always been a social dog, but he seemed to be acting differently with Mona, as if he knew she needed taking care of in that moment. Jasper was once again thankful for the big husky. Karen had never bonded with Snow, and had been happy to leave him behind when she moved, although Taylor had been distraught.

Might as well see if there was anything else he could use, searching through the school in detail. Not much. Summer meant that it was a lot of school supplies, not a whole lot else. The custodial closet had some things, but most were too big to be portable. A mop handle made an okay walking stick for now until he could find something more robust, and there was a pair of work overalls, greasy and stained, but not that much too big for him. An extra layer for the cold nights to come.

The labs had some Bunsen burners, but he couldn't find any fuel for them, and the pop can stove was easier to transport, so he left them where they were. There was also some chalk, a relic from a time before whiteboards. He took as much of it as he could find.

He decided that his best bet was the hunting store he used for his arrows, he drove the extra distance out of town because he liked the place, liked the owners, and they were free with expert advice. The place was far enough away from the city that it might be reasonable to get access to. Next stop after he left the school then.

One issue that wasn't going away was the problem with carrying things. There was nothing in the school to alleviate it, no large trail packs, no wagons, no wheel barrow, he would have taken even that if he could get it. Many of the things the school did have that would be useful were too big to carry, or not worth more than the things he would have to leave behind for them. Already he looked like a walking trash heap when he moved, festooned with objects tied on, strapped on, hanging off each other.

There were computers everywhere, but no power. Again he felt completely isolated. For all Jasper knew this was just Nova Scotia, and the rest of the world was fine, not likely, but there was just no way to tell for sure, no reliable sources of information.

After his walkthrough, he made his way back to Mona. She was still sleeping, no surprise. He settled down to wait, and after a while dozed off himself. He woke to the sound of Mona digging through his bags. She was pulling stuff out, frantic, messy. "Mona, calm down. You are welcome to look through my stuff, but please try to keep it a bit tidy. We might need to book in a hurry. Oh yeah, I don't have any meth".

"What? No, I'm not looking for meth, just looking," she said in a rush, still pulling stuff out of the pack, "I'll put it all back nice and tidy as soon as I'm done".

Jasper didn't care enough to fight about it, so he let her keep going, but kept an eye on where everything was. He noticed a large hockey bag, half hidden under the piles of garbage that seemed to appear around her spontaneously. It wasn't perfect, but it was better than what he had with him.

Finally, Mona ran out of energy. She whimpered and went back to her sleeping bag. The sleeping bag struck Jasper as a tremendous asset, but he still didn't want to touch it. Even if it wasn't infested with anything, it was still disgusting, and the odds it wasn't infested with anything seemed slim. He decided he would just boil it in one of the large pots in the cafeteria and hope they didn't need to run before it dried.

The next few days passed much the same. Mona would wake up for brief periods. Often she would cry, sometimes she would talk about killing herself, how there was no point in her being alive. Jasper waited, knowing that there was no way around this, she had to go through it. Withdrawal from meth was a bitch. He used the first aid kit in the nurse's office to clean up and disinfect her sores, and they started to fade. Her teeth were probably a lost cause, but she began to gain some weight, just a little, and stopped looking like she was already one of the zombies.

Meanwhile, Jasper and Snow kept exploring the school, going through every room in detail. In the teacher's lounge, Jasper found a hoodie that had been left behind by some staff member when they headed out for the summer. The nurse's office was the biggest treasure trove though. It didn't exactly have high-end medical supplies, some over the counter pain medication, disinfectant, thermometers, bandages, scissors, etc. He made sure that Mona was aware of exactly what he found so that she wouldn't decide to ravage through his stuff in the mistaken idea that he might have some drugs, painkillers, in particular, they might ease her withdrawal.

By the time Mona was able to move around again, Jasper was pretty sure he had managed to find everything that was of any use. He said "Look, I'm heading for PEI. My daughter is there, and I need to know if she's alright."

"Kay."

"I'd like you to come with me."

"Kay. Why?"

"Well, more people have a better chance at survival. It means we can take turns keeping watch, things like that."

"I know that. Why should I leave?"

"This place is time limited. If enough of the zombies figure out someone is here it will be a thousand deep, the doors won't stand. There is food, but not that much. Won't be long before we're starving here, hell, you could eat through this kitchen on your own in no time."

"Kay. Makes sense. Stuff to do. Then we leave."

"Alright, what stuff, maybe I can help?"

"Need to get clean. Stink. Clothes stink."

"Alright, I have a plan for that. Come join me in the kitchen."

They washed her clothes in a large pot of boiling water. She stripped naked right there and threw in everything she was wearing. Her body had apparently undergone lots of hardship, but the few days of eating well had started her back on the path to health. While she was still underweight, she didn't look completely emaciated. She noticed Jasper looking, and struck a flirty pose. "Like what you see?"

"You look good, no question."

He was extremely uncomfortable with the situation, not interested at all, but didn't want to hurt her feelings. She kept getting closer to him, invading his space, her naked body so close now that he could feel the warmth of her. Her breath was awful, intolerable.

Jasper stepped back, giving himself a bit of space. "Look, this isn't a good time. Maybe later, not now though, okay?".

"Sure, no worries".

She didn't seem offended, and maybe she was even a tiny bit relieved. She dropped it right away. Jasper did his clothes next. They weren't much better than hers. One little bonus they managed to get from the nurse's office was a pack of toothbrushes and some toothpaste. There were also shower rooms next to the gym, so they got clean in the frigid water as their clothes dried. No towels, but it was still warm out. Finally, they were clean, dry, well fed, well rested, and had all the gear they could carry. It was time to leave. Despite the urgency though Jasper wanted to wait until morning. One last night in relative security and warmth. Mona didn't seem to care.

The next morning dawned bright and early. Since the world ended Jasper found himself going to bed with the end of the day, and get up with first light. Not much could be done in the dark, which left them well rested by first light. It also meant that they measured time by the sun. No schedule other than the one imposed on them by nature.

They started moving very shortly after getting up. A quick breakfast of pancakes with orange juice made up from concentrate before hitting the road. They would not be able to eat like this for a long time, if ever again, so might as well make the most of it.

They started into the early morning light, moving quietly. They were able to see many nearby houses. There were zombies milling around, but they were far away and didn't seem to notice the trio. They kept moving for hours, quickly making it out of the populated areas. Finally, Jasper was out of town, only a week and a bit after he started moving. The forest was dense, with a lot of scrub brush. Jasper was wearing a decent pair of boots, but Mona had an old pair of skate shoes, that were already full of holes, they would need to replace them if the weather got worse. Snow was the happiest Jasper had ever seen him, walking with his pack in the open air, he wore a perpetual doggy grin, tongue hanging out to one side. Jasper was navigating as best he could, but the thick tree cover made it hard to get sun sightings, and neither of them had an analogue watch, time was an estimate. From time to time Jasper would climb a high tree and try to get his bearings. He knew that he wanted to move northwest, probably more north for a little bit.

After a few hours, Jasper spotted a road he knew, which at least gave him a bearing. He was pretty far off course, but it was correctable. There was an undercurrent of panic in his mind, Charlottetown was a long, long way away and every day increased the odds that something would happen to Taylor.

As the day went on Mona started to look tired, stumbling as she walked, slowing down. Jasper had the giant hockey bag, leaving Mona with the small backpack. Lots of her stuff had to be left behind, but none of it was worth anything, most of it was random bits of garbage. Jasper found a spot that was higher than the ground around it and well protected from the elements; then he set to work building a short-term shelter. It was a bunch of pine boughs laid out on the ground with a very small lean to, barely enough room for the three of them - Snow was an added heat source, the big dog always ran hot. Even though the air was warm the ground sucked the heat out of their bodies, they slept on the sleeping bag, unzipped. The gear had to live outside the shelter. The whole thing was hidden deep in a cluster of trees, hard to see from even a couple of feet away, and with the bows laid out the way they were the shelter was nearly invisible. He did take the risk of heating up a small pot of macaroni and cheese and some tea. The pop can stove was small, didn't cast light any distance. The smell of cooking worried him, but the zombies hadn't come to the school, so maybe the smell of food wasn't going to be a problem.

The night passed uneventfully. They didn't talk due to fear of the noise carrying. At first light, they headed out again. Every day was like that for a while, the same drudgery. Water was plentiful, but food was scarce, not much they could forage. The days started to blend.

Mona was always tired, but having an extra set of eyes, an extra pair of hands, it meant the difference between barely surviving, or possibly not surviving, and doing well. Jasper wanted a few more people, of course, hopefully, ones who weren't meth heads who had been on the edge of starving to death before the world ended. Ones with useful skills for this kind of situation. On the bright side, she didn't complain, taking the pain and exhaustion as if it was just a normal part of life, he guessed because for her it always had been.

Clearing the way

If this was home, time to improve the neighbourhood. Zombies don't make good neighbours, and Naomi was determined to spruce things up. As she moved around a few more zombies came out of hidden spots, six of them from what Naomi could see.

She needed to clear all the zombies out, make sure she could move around safely. No point in hiding behind a big fence if you let the zombies stay inside, at least that's what she kept telling herself to keep her nerves steady, prevent herself from falling apart with panic. There was a piece of steel lying on the ground, sharp on one end and about six feet long, not too heavy for her to lift. She pushed the door open a bit and thrust the piece of steel into one of the zombies faces. It didn't do much, just pushed the zombies head back a little, left a torn flap of skin on one cheek. She tried slamming it forward as hard as she could. The zombie bounced back and then came forward again, teeth gnashing.

She had no idea how she was going to kill this thing. She just didn't have the upper body strength or the body weight. She needed leverage, something to brace the zombie against. She really, really didn't want to let them in, but if she didn't do something she was screwed. Most of them were bigger and stronger than her.

She took a chance. She opened the door a tiny bit, enough to let the one zombie in, then pulled it. One of them had his arm trapped, but he was still outside. There were too many for Naomi to deal with all at once, she needed to be able to take her time, be calculated. The one who came in was grabbing for her, so she ducked under his arms, relying on his clumsiness to get around him. She managed that a few more times until she had him with his back to a wall, then she struck. "I got you, motherfucker! Fucking zombie bitch. Eat that shit!" This time the piece of metal bit into him, and she leaned her weight into it. He was struggling forward, impaling himself further on the sharp end. Eventually, her hundred pounds of body weight did the trick; she pushed the metal through the zombies face, deep into his brain. She was exhausted, and there were still five to go.

The next one was harder to get inside. Naomi pushed the door, but it barely moved, the zombies trying to get in were pushing against the door, keeping it closed, keeping them from getting to her. Thank god they were too stupid to pull. She had to use the piece of steel as a lever, and then grab it back as the zombies started to reach for it. Two made it in before she was able to get the door closed, fuck. She had to come up with something else, fast. She managed to swing her piece of steel at the closer one's head, hitting it in the temple. It fell, still moving but off balance, giving her time and space to do her moving around trick with the other one. Again she managed to pin it between her and the wall, slamming it harder, panic making adrenaline pulse through her body. Its skull cracked and it fell. After she turned back to the first one, it was much closer than she had anticipated. This one was a fat woman, twice Naomi's size. It got one hand on her, so she dropped to the ground, sliding between its legs. The zombie fell, folded in half. As soon as it was down, she swung the piece of steel into its head, a high overhand arc. The piece of metal smashed into the zombie, slamming its skull back into the concrete floor of the building, shattering its skull and laying it to rest.

Naomi was exhausted, her reserves spent. She collapsed, shaking on the floor, her belly was protesting her exertion, nausea flowed over her in waves. She was afraid she was going to shit her pants and puke at the same time. She lay there for a long time, taking gulping breaths and hoping something would change, that the zombies that were left would get distracted and go somewhere else, that someone would come to save her, something, anything. Nobody did, and when she calmed down enough to get back up, she grabbed a bite to eat and picked up the piece of metal again.

It took her twelve hours to deal with the six zombies. She took breaks, sometimes hours long, came up with new strategies to get the door open, get one inside, and get it closed again. There was some rope holding one of the bags together, so she used that once she found it, slipping it over a zombies neck, ducking behind it, and lashing it to a pillar. That was the last one, and the easiest. Clearing them from her little hut took another few hours. She dragged them out to the middle of the tarmac; then she left them there. The crows started picking at them, ignoring the ones that were still moving outside the fence.

The airport was starting to get busy. So far the zombies were still outside the fence, but they were building up against the chain link. Every once in a while Naomi would try to clear a few away from the fence. Her arms had trouble with the task though; she didn't have the strength to take out very many. She would stab a few and find her arms trembling with the strain, and the time she spent by the fence would attract more. The chain link wasn't showing signs of stress yet, but it was leaning heavily. The constant moaning and the sound of the links moving under the zombies were starting to get to her. She was lonely. Sometimes she talked to the zombies; sometimes she cursed at them. They didn't seem to care either way.

She didn't want to move yet, there was food here, more than she could carry. The luggage was valuable too. Several luggage vans were parked on the tarmac, and most of them had at least a partial load. The planes were death traps. She could see movement in the small windows when the light was right. They had become giant steel tubes of zombies.

Naomi set up an exit point. She ran a ramp up to the top of the fence, made of loose boards. If you were inside it was a quick and easy escape, just needed a little bit of coordination, but did nothing for you if you were outside. Then she did that three more times, in different spots.

None of the luggage vans contained a backpack, at least not a decent one. There was a small Dora the Explorer backpack, bigger than what she had, but the quality was low, so she left it. The luggage gave her something to do, more than anything else. Sometimes it was frustrating. There was a gun safe, locked. No doubt it had a handgun inside, prepped for travel. She couldn't get it open, despite trying again and again. She smashed it with her piece of pointy steel, but the steel bent and the safe was barely scratched. She tried dropping cinder blocks on it. They turned to powder and the finish on the safe got slightly less shiny. In the end, she gave up on it.

One day, not far into her stay, the fence finally went. It was at a gate; the padlock failed under the strain. At least she heard the fence scraping the ground, giving her some warning. Suddenly there were hundreds of zombies inside with her. They were still a few hundred meters away, so she grabbed her little backpack and started to run. The exit point worked as planned, she dropped the boards behind her, closing off the way over the fence. The zombies followed her, slamming into the fence and piling up against it, snarling and moaning, mouths hungry, always hungry. She gave them the finger and walked into the forest.

Meet me behind the wood pile

After a week of journeying Mona and Jasper finally saw another living person. They were coming up on a lumber yard, stacks of wood piled up to the sky. It was remote, a small office and the mill building the only structures in sight. A young black woman was crouched behind a stack of lumber, a piece of scrap steel in her hand, hiding from a group of a dozen or so zombies. A dozen was a lot to deal with, and there were no clear choke points in the lumber yard, just stacks and stacks of wood with wide spaces between them. Jasper moved in to help the stranger out. He didn't think Mona was going to be much use, she was exhausted, and as she didn't have a weapon, he expected her to stay back. Instead, she grabbed his crowbar as he headed down and following close behind. Snow could be counted on to disable at least one of them.

One of the creatures spotted Jasper as he closed, a big man dressed like a lumberjack, it started in his direction. He couldn't see the woman anymore, but some of the zombies were still focused on her. About half of them followed the lumberjack. Coming for him. He tried to make it to a lumber pile so he could have his back to something, but they reached him well before he got there. The first one grabbed for him. Jasper swung his sword up in an underhand blow that took one of the zombies arms just at the elbow. Jasper followed it up with a push kick to its stomach. The zombie was too big, too heavy. It barely moved. Jasper managed to push it back just a little bit, enough to get the sword in position for a head shot. The blade cut deep, and the creature dropped. That left five, and they were in between him and the lumber pile, but he realised that the commotion had dragged the rest in. Meant he had to deal with all eleven.

Mona closed on one of the trailing zombies and spiked the back of its skull with a single efficient motion. The creature dropped like a stone. She moved on to the next and smashed it across the temple. Another hit, another kill. She had four down before one of them noticed her. As soon it turned towards her she ran the other way, moving fast for once. A couple peeled off to chase her. She moved in the direction of the lumber pile the black woman was hiding behind, keeping just ahead of them.

Snow grabbed one of them by the leg and wrestled it to the ground, jaws clamped around dead flesh. It started trying to bite him, but he was good at avoiding teeth, and the zombies weren't smart. He had it locked up in seconds, lying on its stomach with his teeth in the back of its neck. Snow never let the zombie's teeth get near him.

Jasper wished he had some form of armour. Four zombies were enough that if he couldn't pick the ground it was hard, almost too much for him. They moved slowly, they were weak, but numbers are hard to account for. He started swinging the sword. Generally, that would make an opponent back up. This wasn't a typical situation though. The zombies didn't care if they took damage. His sword sliced through the zombie's stomach, the creature didn't even flinch. The zombies kept closing on him, not giving him room to move, to breathe. He managed to punch his sword straight up through one of the creature's jaws and into its brain, but that meant his sword was trapped, pulling down out of his hand. He dropped it because he couldn't get it free fast enough and slammed a slim girl in the chest. Luckily alive she hadn't weighed very much, and dead weighed even less. She flew back and fell on her back, trying to stumble to her feet. He push kicked another one and it went back and down. The last one that was on him was pushing hard, but he was able to get his knife free from his belt. He swung a haymaker with the knife to the temple and felt the blade bite deep. The creature fell and he moved on to the small girl. He could just see Mona at the edge of the woodpile, moving fast. A piece of sharp metal flew into view, hitting one of the pursuing zombies square in the face. The zombie dropped like a stone, its own momentum adding force to the hit, destroying its head. Mona stopped and spun, swinging the pry bar at the end of her arm. It hit the zombie in the shoulder, a minor miscalculation of position. The creature was thrown off balance and hit the ground hard. The other woman slammed the big piece of metal down on the creature, hitting both arms at once. If it had been human that would have ended things, both arms broken, bones sticking through its forearms.

Jasper had to keep focus, stop being distracted by the other skirmish. He had enough to deal with. Rounding on the small girl, he kicked her down as she tried to get up. He didn't feel safe taking the knife to her, so he just kicked down on her head, again and again. Finally, her skull cracked, and he kept going. The last one started to close on him. It looked like it had been one of the lumber yard employees. A big man in a hard hat and an orange vest. Jasper moved in on it, meeting it half way. He swung a low roundhouse kick to the creatures leading leg. It fell, leg knocked off the ground, and Jasper dropped on it, knife straight out. His blade bit into its jaw, breaking through the roof of its mouth and up into its brain. Mona smashed her pry bar down on her zombies head. Finally, it stopped. She moved over to where Snow was holding the last one down. She used the straight end of the pry bar to catch the final zombie in the temple. It went limp, and Snow anxious go.

The black woman was younger than she had looked from a distance. She was dirty, clothes torn and stained from life on the road, scratched up and bleeding from dozens of tiny cuts, but no visible bites and her clothing hadn't been the most practical to start with, so it didn't leave a whole lot of her body hidden. Her shoes were the most reasonable part, but they looked too big for her, so he was pretty sure the original shoes had matched the outfit, a pair of short shorts and a crop top, both very tight. Her hair was cut short, kind of a pixie cut.

"I'm Jasper. Nice to meet you."

"Naomi, charmed. Lovely day what?" she replied in a very obviously fake, very chipper British accent. When she spoke, she seemed even younger. Jasper thought she was probably still in her teens.

Mona piped in, "Mona. Hi." in her usual rapid mumbled monotone.

"We should probably get moving. That much noise might have attracted some attention," Jasper said.

"Just let me grab my shit". Naomi walked between the lumber piles and grabbed a small backpack.

"Hey, you know where we are?" Jasper asked. He had a vague idea, but it was very vague.

"I was staying at a building by the airport last few days, had to book out of there. Headed west. We should be close to Elmsdale right now. Easier to tell once night hits."

"Elmsdale is good. I buy archery gear from a place near there... Would be good to see if it's accessible. They have guns too, ammo, all of it. The town's pretty small too, might not have that many zombies".

"Okay, more or less North from here".

Naomi had a watch on, she held her arm up and lined up the sun, then started walking. "You coming? Fuck. Keep up."

Jasper liked her right away.

As they got into deeper brush, they relaxed a bit, talking as they went. "What do you do for a living Naomi? I'm a programmer, or I guess I was."

"Waitress, at a Caribbean place. Auntie ran it. I was going back to school in the fall."

"Didn't work. Stayed home. Mostly got stoned. Surprise, zombies."

"None of us are badass commandos then. I'm trained in survival, at least a bit. Did a bunch of martial arts too, so I'm not completely useless. Either of you any good with a bow? If we rely on my aim we spend most of our time trying to find the arrows I fire deep into the woods, far, far away from anything I'm trying to hit."

"No, never shot no bow. ; the like a white girl? Where I gonna shoot arrows at?"

"Yes. Compound. That one's too big for me. I'm a good shot. Those arrows are no good."

Mona and Naomi kept giving each other sideways looks, staying a bit away from each other. The tension between them was thick, almost palpable. Jasper had revamped his initial appraisal of Mona. He had assumed that she started hiding when the zombies hit and that her survival was down to blind luck. Apparently, she could fight. Maybe he would have to find out more about her skills, not assume so much.

After talking for a while, he started to get a picture of each of them. Mona was still reticent to talk about herself, and it was hard to understand her when she did speak. The quiet mumble that was her standard mode of speech was difficult to make out. From what he could guess she had been in a trailer with a few other people. One of them had started to come down, but Mona was still flying and far from sleep. The sleeping girl had turned and then got up to start munching on Mona's boyfriend. Mona smashed her into a pulp with an ashtray. By then her boyfriend had turned, and another one of the tweakers had turned as well, she didn't see him get bitten or anything. He was eating the last girl who was with them, so Mona grabbed all the meth that was left and lit the curtains on fire. Then she took off and slammed the door behind her. Way, way tougher than Jasper had thought.

Naomi was heading for either Cape Breton or PEI. She was only 17. Jasper was impressed by Naomi. Her apparent intelligence and quick thinking at odds with her youth.

The light was starting to fade, pink tinges showing on the horizon, twilight stealing in, like a thief, taking their time from them. They needed to find secure shelter; the area was too exposed. Mona pointed out a small cluster of houses, barely visible through the trees. A group of McMansions, part of the recent urban sprawl. "Good call, probably not too many people," Jasper said.

"Crazy houses. Never been anywhere that big."

"I spent the first day after the zombies in a place like that, empty. It was alright, but not great. Ugly as hell though, for some reason they had parts of it painted bright pink. They aren't all they are cracked up to be. Give me a house with some personality any day."

"Better than a trailer."

"Yeah, I guess."

They staked out the closest house, an enormous boxy place with no architectural features, covered in brick facade. The kind of place Jasper's neighbourhood was full of, on a larger scale. A quick look through all the ground floor windows didn't reveal any movement inside, living or dead, and there was no vehicle in the driveway. The place wasn't new construction though, just empty. There was a swimming pool, currently full of leaves and random bits of detritus. A small stream ran behind the property. The front door was unlocked.

They decided to chance it. The house still seemed to be empty. There was a dog dish with food still in it just inside the door; Snow went right to it. The water bowl next to it was half full, but the water was covered in a layer of scum. The sound of buzzing flies filled the house, and the smell permeated their senses, drowning out everything else. Not the smell of the dead, but the smell of rotting food, left long in the heat. They drew their weapons and entered the kitchen. The table had four places set. All the places had food, half eaten, covered in mould. The plates were writhing, layers of maggots wriggling and crawling under thick green fuzz.

"Let's check the place," Jasper said, "stick together, none of that horror movie shit. It'll take way longer if one of us gets killed."

One of the upstairs rooms had the door closed, and there was a steady thumping on the door. Jasper drew his sword while Naomi handled the door. It pushed inward, creaking slowly on dusty hinges. She opened it and then jumped back. A small figure shambled out towards them, A little girl, around four or five years old. They couldn't see any wounds on her. Other than the grey skin and blank eyes she could have been just getting ready for pre-school. Too bright clothes, although stained now. There was some crusted blood around her mouth, but no apparent wound to account for it, it wasn't hers.

Jasper took her head off with one swing. The angle was wrong thanks to her height, so half her shoulder came off with it. Her small bones barely slowed the blade, leaving her arm attached by a small strip of muscle and flesh after the blade was through. They went into the room, clearly a child's room and stripped the bright pink sheets off the bed. They covered the little girl with her sheets and put her back in her bed.

The rest of the house was clear, light, warm and stinky, but clear. In the basement, they found a generator with a full gas tank, power for the night. They needed to cover the windows, use as little light as possible, the water would work though, they could take a shower, wash their clothes - unparalleled luxury. The house had some things they could use as well, A pop up five person tent, four sleeping bags, although only two of them were adult size, which was okay because Mona already had one, and two large camping packs. Various other camping gear was in the basement as well, high-end yuppie stuff. It wasn't what Jasper would have purchased for himself, but that was mostly because he couldn't afford it. It was all portable, the kind of gear you would take if you had to trek into the camp site, perfect for what they needed.

"Well, glad we picked this place," Jasper said, "It's funny, the next house down the road might have had none of this stuff, choosing this place might mean the difference between life and death. So, which rooms do you guys want?"

"Let's stick together. The big bedroom. The bed looks amazing. So comfy." Naomi said.

None of them was willing to sleep away from the group, just in case, but Naomi wasn't used to snuggling close overnight, something Mona and Jasper had started doing out of necessity. The king size bed meant they could have some space and all be comfortable. The next morning they packed up the camping gear as best they could. There was even a small bit of trail food. Freeze dried meals and vacuum packed trail mix. Enough to last them several days with proper rationing. So far hunger had been a minor problem, and water had been easy. Shelter was their biggest issue, one that was now solved.

Once again Naomi was invaluable. Navigating through the woods like she was using a GPS. The going was slow, but by late that afternoon they came in sight of Elmsdale. It was a small town, not many people even when there wasn't a zombie apocalypse going on. Most of the population seemed to be out on the street, shambling around and looking for neighbours to eat.

"We need to create a distraction," Jasper said, "draw them out of town, get their numbers down enough that we can grab what we need. Even so, we will have to be quick about it."

Naomi said, "You got a plan?"

"Yeah, I read a book one time where the characters set off a car alarm, pulled all the zombies to the car, gave them time to get what they needed. Figured we'd do something like that. The highway goes right past town, should be some cars on it. There are a lot of commuters there normally, at least a few of them should be in range."

"Risky. Whoever sets off the alarm gonna have a shitload of zombies chasing them. Also, I just had a real conversation where I said that. This is too fucking weird."

"Yeah, I think I should do it, I used to run every day, should be able to get away from the car before any zombies get too close."

It took about two minutes for the plan to start to go wrong. Jasper found a car that was a decent fit, but the alarm wouldn't trigger. Some checking and he realized it was a dead battery, the keys were in the ignition and the lights were on. He found another one, but the path wasn't clear to the woods. He hit it anyway and booked as fast as he could as soon as the alarm started. He ran to the rendezvous point and joined the women. A few zombies seemed to be curious, but after a couple of minutes of the alarm going off they started to drift away, the noise didn't seem to entice them at all.

Time for a new plan. They found sheltered spot to talk and started trying to come up with one. Jasper had one more idea, but it wasn't one he liked. "So, I have a thought. Kind of wish I didn't."

Naomi turned to him. "What is it?"

"I start running, get them following me. Head out to the highway. There's a spot I can jump off, get to safety that they can't follow me. It's high but manageable, and there's guard rails, high enough to keep the zombies from following. It's a bit of a risk, but not too bad."

"Well, that's a shit sandwich."

"Yeah, but it needs to be done. We need weapons, the store has weapons."

Mona, as usual, sat back and watched them discuss options. It was rare that she put her two cents in, seemingly content to go with the flow.

It was getting late, Jasper wanted as much daylight for his plan as possible, so they made camp for the night and went over last minute details. Getting to the store wasn't going to be a problem, there weren't a whole lot of roads in Enfield.

Morning came early. Jasper popped out of bed as soon as the light hit his eyes. He hadn't slept much. "Well, nothing for it. Guess I'm playing bait now. Have fun ladies, do wait up..."

"We have this. Don't die." Mona said.

Jasper made his way into town. He left most of his gear with the women, even his sword. The process of jumping off the highway was going to take all of his skill, and any extra weight meant disaster. He felt vulnerable, almost naked. "Come on mother fuckers, dinners on!" He started yelling while running through the street. The zombies reached for him, their numbers increasing by the moment.

After a few blocks, he had a large following. There were hundreds and hundreds of them, reaching out for him, trying to grab him. A bunch had started to come together ahead of him, apparently blocking his way. He kicked off one of the walls, and then kicked off another one, gaining about ten feet of air, enough to sail over the heads of the zombies. He landed in a shoulder roll, coming out of it at a full run. The zombies turned and started following him. He had about half the population of Enfield chasing him. He was also out of town. Ahead of him, there were a few lone zombies, but the road was wide and he wasn't really worried about them. He slowed to a casual run and started down the road.

There were cars, a fair number of them. The road would be impassable to anything larger than a motorbike, but it was all right for a pedestrian. At one point, however, there was a car that had spun across the road, the hood touching the side wall, the rear in the main line of cars. Jasper was worried about that one because he was still too close to town to lose the zombies, so he passed through the middle of the cars. A hand grabbed his ankle from under one of the cars, taking him off his feet. He reacted fast, going into a shoulder roll and right back to his feet, but slammed off the side of a minivan. Dazed for a moment, he let the lead zombie almost reach him, got it back together and started running again, faster this time, zig-zagging back through the cars until he was back on the clear area on the left shoulder of the road.

Jasper was starting to get winded. He was almost at the spot he had picked out, so he kept going. His lungs burned, and he had a stitch in his right side, not much of one but it was unpleasant. He kept pushing, kept running. Finally, he made it to his spot. It was higher than he thought, and the landing was anything but level. Didn't matter, he was committed. It was either make the jump or get torn to shreds when he got too tired to stay ahead of the horde. He turned and launched himself up and over the wall. The ground below sloped up the further it was from the road, he tried to get as much horizontal distance as he could.

He got his legs under him and landed in an awkward uphill roll. He felt a hard smack against his head and a sharp pain in his left arm, then he was back on his feet. He started running back towards town, but his head began to swim, filling with dizziness and nausea, so he slowed to a walk.

The haul

Mona and Naomi waited until the zombies thinned out on the street.

"Let's go. Grab us some guns."

"Shut. Up."

"What the fuck? What's your problem bitch. You don't tell me to shut up."

"You talk too loud. Zombies. Don't wanna get eaten." Mona said, low and fast as always.

"Alright. You and me gonna have words later though."

"K. Quiet now."

They walked the rest of the way in silence, glaring at each other as they went.

Hnatiuk's, the hunting store, was a small place right on the main road. The door had a note pinned to it. It read "If you can read this, the door is unlocked, come inside, take what you need. We're all in this together".

They entered the store. There were racks and racks of guns, all still there. Not only that, whoever had unlocked the door had unlocked every display case, storage area, etc. The register was open and full of cash. The ammo had some empty spots, but there were many, many boxes. There were knives, bows, guns, arrowheads, etc. It was exactly what Jasper had promised, with the added bonus of being set up for anyone who wanted to come take what they needed. Naomi felt a burst of hope wash over her, maybe humanity wasn't completely screwed.

They filled up bags with weapons and ammo, still in silence. Naomi felt almost guilty about stripping the place, but survival won out, so she kept going, grabbing as much as she thought she could carry. Mona had more, a lot more. A bag bulging and overflowing with weaponry, two bows strapped across her chest, two full quivers of arrows.

"You forget we need to carry camping gear too?" Naomi said, "No way we can use that much shit."

"Better to have guns. Can get food with guns. Bows too. I can shoot."

"K, whatever. I ain't carrying your shit though."

"K. Don't care."

They left the store, Mona staggering under the weight of all her weapons. The bag looked like it was larger than her. Naomi spotted Jasper heading towards them. Somehow Snow had caught up to him and was trailing a pace or two behind. The big dog freaked her out, so quiet, not mean, but not friendly either. He was a shadow. Jasper didn't look so good, there was blood on his shirt, dripping down his side. He was pale, almost green, and he was swaying back and forth as he walked.

"Fuck. Jasper, you alright? What happened? You get bit?"

"No, fucked up the jump. Landed bad. I think I hit my head. I'm okay though."

"Fuck you are. You bleeding like a motherfucker. Let's go. Back to the camp, we gotta check you out."

Back at camp, Jasper started pulling off his shirt, but it was caught on something. Slowly, gingerly, the women helped him pull it away from his side. They found a stick poking through his shirt into his stomach. It wasn't very thick, but it was rough and the wood was still green, dirt and moss caked the bark.

Mona grabbed the stick and started to pull. Jasper grabbed her hand. "Look, it does need to come out... but if we just pull without thinking about it I might bleed out. We need to clean the wound and be ready to stop the bleeding. Normally it's best to get to a hospital, but they don't seem to be running these days. Have you ever sutured a wound before?"

"Nope. Never. Will try... you can be my first."

"OK. I can talk you through most of it. Shouldn't be too bad. Man, I don't feel so good."

They used the camp stove to boil some water, sterilized some gauze strips, and set some water aside so they could use it to clean the wound.

They also got some extra bandages to wrap the wound. Everything laid out on a newly sterilized cloth. It was pretty rough, they did everything possible to prevent infection, but conditions were what they were.

Naomi did all the prep, she was precise and methodical, but Mona was going to do the sewing. Naomi didn't feel confident in her ability to close the wound. Much as she hated to admit it, Mona was much, much stronger. None of them had a clue what they were doing. Jasper had some first aid training, but with his head swimming, he wasn't much use.

"Ready?" Mona said, grabbing the stick.

"No, give me a minute. Okay, no, wait... okay, go."

Mona pulled, the stick popped out with a spurt of blood. It was longer than they had thought, most of it buried in Jasper's abdomen. Naomi pressed a cloth to the wound as soon as the stick was clear, putting her weight into it. The blood slowed, pooling in the cloth, while Mona got sterile strips to clean the wound with. She poured rubbing alcohol over the wound, then poured sugar from a bunch of sugar packets into the wound. Time to sew it shut, she grabbed a needle, held it over the flame from the camp stove for a moment, a final step, and started sewing Jasper's flesh shut. It took three stitches, and it was ugly. Naomi poured more alcohol over the wound and packed it with gauze. Finally she wound gauze around Jasper's stomach, binding it as tight as she dared.

Jasper managed to stay still for the whole process, then he turned over and puked his guts out.

Wounded, nearly dead

The next few days were a write-off. Jasper was raving, incoherent. He insisted that they walk, that making it to Charlottetown was important, that they couldn't stop, not even for a day. He could barely stand, and threw up often.

"You can't walk, idiot." Naomi said, "Lie down, let us take care of you."

"Can't. Gotta make it to Taylor, she needs me."

"Yeah, we gonna get there. You keep trying to walk you ain't going nowhere. You gonna fall down and die, then Mona and me gotta put a knife through your brain, how that help Taylor?"

There were a lot more zombies around, wandering the woods. Mostly solo. Naomi got fairly competent at wielding Jasper's sword, and of course, Mona was able to pick up any weapon and wreak mayhem. She seemed to have a talent for killing, possibly one that she picked up well before the end of the world. They didn't train with the guns because the noise might attract zombies, they did practice with the bows, however. Jasper's old arrows were only useful for targets, as the bullet points were no good for killing, too blunt. They were glued to the shafts, so they couldn't even swap those out. Instead, they fired them into trees, hills, whatever they could find. Jasper kept urging them to move on whenever he woke up, then he didn't wake up for too long and they got scared. His head was burning up, a high fever. They had some meagre medical supplies, nothing for this though. Mona got cold water from a stream, as much as she could carry, and started trying to cool him down. Finally, Naomi had enough and decided to try and find some antibiotics. There was a grocery store near the highway, far from the populated areas of town, or at least as far as one could get in a town this size. The moon was nearly full, the night was bright, cloudless and hot, one of those summer nights full of humidity. She grabbed a bow, Jasper's sword, and the pry bar.

Mona handed her a handgun "Gun. Take it."

"Makes too much noise, I don't want all the zombies chasing me."

"So don't shoot. Better have it, not need it."

"Alright, thanks." Naomi was touched, She would have said until that moment that Mona would be glad if she was eaten. The small woman was hard to read.

She left Mona with Jasper, keeping his temperature down as much as she could. Sick people made her uncomfortable, always had. Snow was lying next to Jasper, whimpering from time to time and licking his master's hand.

Naomi kept low to the ground and moved quietly. Not all of the zombies had made it back to town, but a lot had, the streets were crawling with the undead. Naomi slipped between a pair of houses and into the grocery store parking lot. The doors on the store were closed and the lot only had three cars in it. This chain always had pharmacies in store. Naomi made it right to the door without attracting any attention, then she pried the doors open. It took all her strength, pushing her body against the bar again and again, and the bar made a horrible screeching sound as she leaned her full weight into it one final time. Shuffling steps echoed from the parking lot, making the hairs on the back of her neck stand up in fear. She slipped in between the doors and pulled them shut behind her. The lock was broken, but the door shut flush, no handles. She didn't think the zombies would be able to figure out how to pull the doors apart, so she turned her focus to the next set. They were sensor doors, and she managed to pull them open easily.

The pharmacy was in the middle of the store. It had a gate down over the counter and a locked door. She pushed the bar in under the gate and jammed it up as hard as she could, then slammed it down with all of her weight. Nothing. Again. Again. Finally, it broke and the gate popped open. Naomi hopped the counter and moved into the pharmacy area.

There were rows and rows of bottles. Some had pills, others had powders, liquids, etc. Some had labels, others just had bar codes. Many of the drugs were stored in drawers, again labelled with bar codes. There was a scanner gun, no use without power, but hidden half under the register was a lookup book, giving the codes and the related drug and dose.

There was also a book of drug interactions, which seemed like it might be useful. They were going to have to figure this out from scratch, Naomi knew next to nothing about prescription pharmaceuticals. She had a sneaking suspicion that Mona might know more about a few of them, mostly the pain killers. She started taking pills, writing down the type based on the book. She took a whole bunch of everything and hoped. The drugs she did know about weren't there, in fact, there was a sign saying the pharmacy didn't stock Oxycodone.

Naomi also spotted a clothing department. She was being eaten alive by insects, her short shorts and crop top not providing a lot of protection. She picked out some pants, they didn't have anything cute, but ugly and not eaten beat the hell out of cute and covered in insect bites, so she picked out a couple of pairs of cargo pants, some underwear, a few decent shirts, even some socks and a pair of shoes that fit. Not the greatest shoes, but no worse than the ones she was wearing, and being her size made a world of difference. She hit seasonal as well, they had fall stuff in, some bug spray still kicking around on a back shelf though. There were a few other camping related items, nothing big ticket, or high end, she was able to stock up on alcohol canisters for the camp stove and a set of walkie talkies, long range ones, some sort of hunting season special. Mostly it was back to school stuff, lying out for a group of students who would never arrive.

She made her way into the back area of the store, away from the shelves and into the boxes. The area was lined floor to ceiling with shelving, boxes on most of it. It felt claustrophobic, close, dangerous. Naomi drew her sword and started walking to the rear door, or at least where she thought the door was. She heard a noise from behind, a soft sound, so she turned. There was a zombie coming up from behind, a large woman wearing a smock. Naomi struck fast and hard, not wasting any time. The sword bit into the zombie's skull, and stopped. She didn't have enough force behind the blade, and now it was wedged in the bone. She turned to run, better to lose the sword than her life, but there was another zombie closing in from behind her, leaving her trapped. The woman with the sword in her head was closing, pressing forward.

Naomi grabbed the sword hilt and pushed, leaning all of her weight into the weapon. The zombie staggered back a tiny bit, then a bit more. It was too slow, the other zombie would be on her long in a moment. She ran to her left, dragging the zombies head around with her, and leaned back, using her weight to try and pull the sword free. It came out suddenly, knocking Naomi off balance. She landed on her back on the cement floor, the wind knocked out of her instantly. The large female zombie kept coming, black ichor leaking from her skull. She reached down for Naomi, hand clawlike and outstretched, mouth impossibly wide. Naomi thrust the sword up in desperation, just as the zombie dropped down. The sword slammed into the zombie's mouth, using the zombie's own weight as it fell down. The blade passed through the zombie's skull, and it kept dropping, no longer animated. Naomi scrambled under the dead bodies weight, trying to get herself free before the other zombie reached her. She couldn't see anything for a moment, her face covered by the dead woman's breasts.

With a lot of pushing she managed to get her face free, just as the other zombie, this one a teenage boy with shaggy brown hair and dead grey eyes, reached her. It was reaching for her legs, mouth open. No other choice then, she pushed her right hand under the dead woman's bulk, reaching the handgun in her waist band, and pulled it out. The gun caught on the dead woman's smock, so she pulled harder, as hard as she could, every muscle straining. Finally, a tearing sound and the gun pulled free. She pulled the trigger, and nothing happened. Safety. Fuck.

She flipped the safety off and fired, hitting the zombie in the shoulder, knocking it slightly off course. A second shot, this time she hit its head, and it dropped. Her ears were ringing from the gunshots, she couldn't hear anything else. "Fuck. I'm deaf. Motherfucker."

She finally managed to get herself pulled out from under the dead woman, and she headed back into the store. The shot might have brought zombies around back, to her escape route.

There were a couple dozen zombies out front, a parking lot full. None of them had managed to get the front door open. Naomi sat down and threw up, the adrenaline dump gone, her body was overcome with exhaustion.

She grabbed a couple of cans of coconut water and downed them, not caring that they were warm.

After a few minutes, she had her breath back, the shaking had mostly stopped. She still wanted to lie down and sleep, but Jasper needed the meds, and sooner would be better from how he looked before she left. She got up, got her legs under control, and shot through the front window of the store. The noise echoed through the dark store, the crashing of glass hitting the ground almost as loud. She turned and started running, as the zombies came through the now open front of the store.

She slammed through the door to the back, turned, and locked it. The store would be full of zombies, and hopefully, any that had made it to the back were now going to the front, following the noise and the horde.

The back door stood there, steel, solid, menacing. Out there could be anything. If her gambit worked, a short run to the forest. If it had failed, maybe dozens of zombies.

"Oh well, no time like the present" she mumbled under her breath, and then carefully opened the door. Nothing visible behind the store, so she hurried out of the open and into the woods on the other side of the parking lot.

One of the zombies caught sight of her as she went, others followed. By the time she was in the trees there were a dozen zombies following her. She cast her eyes around for a defensible spot. Naomi didn't have much left in her body, the coconut water had helped, but only a tiny bit. There was a very short cliff, maybe three or four feet, and the ground narrowed in a kind of V heading towards it. There was a large tree at the apex of the V. She ran for it, trying to get up the cliff before they reached her, drawing her sword as she went.

The first creature reached her just as she made it to the tree. She swung the sword down on top of its head, but the angle wasn't right, and she ended up biting deep into its left shoulder. The creatures left arm came off, but it still kept biting at her, and the sword was wedged. She pushed one leg against its chest and pulled. The blade came free and she bounced back against the trunk. Movies made it look so easy, she had no idea swords got stuck so often.

She needed to be more cautious, less fancy. She slammed the point of the blade into its face. The blade smashed through and into the brain. The creature dropped, but there was another one right behind it and one to the right as well. She chopped off a leg on the one on the right, then managed to sever the head of the other one. three down, nine to go. The one without a leg was still coming, crawling towards her though. She came down on the back of its head and it stopped moving. The next wave had three. One of them was a toddler. Horrific, but useful. She kicked it in the head and it rolled down hill, giving her more time to deal with the others.

The next few minutes got lost in a red haze. Lift the sword, thrust, swing, chop. Finally, she brought the blade down point first into the skull of the toddler. The hill leading up to her perch was covered in gore and death. Limbs hacked off, heads severed. She wanted armour if she was going to keep doing this. Too many close calls in too short a span of time.

She crept back to camp slowly, staying out of sight of the zombies. Her hearing gradually came back as she went.

Mona said, "Thought you got eaten," as soon as she got back.

"Nope, sorry. I'm still alive. Thanks though, the gun was good. You a'ight"

"Glad. Pills."

Well, the woman was probably never going to be friendly, but maybe a friend anyway.

They went through the pills together, using the book to identify what they had. Mona seemed disappointed that there weren't any serious narcotics, but had a pretty decent knowledge of medication. She grabbed a few pills and gave them to Jasper. They had a hard time getting him to swallow, but they didn't exactly have a lot of other options.

By that night Jasper's fever was down. He woke up for a bit and they managed to get him to keep down some food. The wound was still hot to the touch, but the redness was down a bit. They also kept pushing water on him, keeping him hydrated. "I feel like shit."

"You look like shit. Thought you was pale before, now you look like you been bleached."

"Thanks, love you too."

The great hunter

By the next day, Jasper was capable of sitting up. Still not walking, but not on the edge of death. Over the next few days, he recovered strength, until he was finally able to get going again. They were low on food by that point - of course. None of them was willing to go back into Elmsdale though, so they decided to chance it and headed off into the mainland.

As they travelled they tried some frequency scanning on the walkie talkies. For a long time they got nothing, then a scratchy voice came over the line. They couldn't figure out what it was saying, but the talkies only had a max range of about fifty kilometres, and likely a lot less in practice, so whoever it was, they were close. They kept on that channel, getting short bursts of voice, and followed the path that made the quick squawks louder and clearer.

Eventually, they managed to make out some of the words on the channel. There were several voices, mostly male, all giving quick focused commands or replies. It sounded military, but the talkies they were using were definitely civilian models.

"We need food. I'm going to do a bit of hunting," Jasper said, grabbing a small hunting rifle from the packs. He was still weak, but functional. Also, he was hungry. They were very low on food. There was only so much they could carry and none of them were feeling up to another population centre.

Jasper found a deer trail and followed it, looking for traces of deer to shoot. Several hours later he decided to try for something more realistic. He spotted a squirrel, fired off a shot, and then cursed as the squirrel took off, intact but scared.

They knew that they only realistically got one shot before having to move on. Who knew if the zombies would come to that noise or not... they left the area as fast as they could.

They kept stumbling into bogs as they travelled, the land suddenly turning into a sodden slog, every step trying to drag them down. The bogs were full of biting insects and thorn bushes, tearing at their skin, tearing holes in their clothes. The landscape was dotted with bogs of all sizes; often they were the only way through an area, cliffs forcing their path.

Naomi kept them to their path though, confident in her sense of direction.

"Hey, Naomi, how the hell do you always know where we are?"

"I was with this fine boy named Tyrell. He was beautiful, but he smart too. Boy was in university, doing astronomy. He used to take me to the telescope, to look at the stars. It was cool, felt like being up in space, way the fuck away from my life. I started getting really into it and shit, reading about stars and constellations and all that. Once I found out you could use them for directions, I was hooked. Read all kinda shit about astronomy, navigation, all of it. Guess I always liked maps too. Mostly I wanted to get out of Nova Scotia, thought it would be easier if I knew where I was going."

"Makes sense"

"Anyways, Tyrell, he got this sweet job, but meant he had to move away, down to South America, some observatory in the mountains. He bought me a telescope before he left."

"Why didn't you go with him?"

"I was in grade ten. You can't take no jailbait to another country. I miss that boy."

Jasper found himself falling into a deep depression. He didn't know how long they'd been travelling, he'd lost days to the fever, and travel was painfully slow. Snow kept him going, not just because of his tireless friendship and enthusiasm, but because he provided a link to Taylor, reminding him of why he had to keep moving, of what this journey was about. Taylor had named the big husky when Jasper first got him, refusing to even consider a more conventional name. The delays, the lack of progress though, they were sapping Jasper's motivation. The lack of calories was also taking a toll, leaving him weak and short of stamina.

He knew how to trap, but that involved waiting a few days and checking the traps over and over again. He refused to set aside the time needed, driving himself harder and harder as he started to fail.

It's a small world after all

They kept walking North West, and the signal kept getting clearer. Jasper was pushing hard, trying to go further every day, trying to make do with less, fewer calories, less sleep, fewer breaks. Finally, after the signal had gotten fairly strong, Mona fell over. She was walking, and then she was lying on the ground, eyes closed. Her breathing was shallow and her pulse was rapid. Jasper tried to remember if he had seen her drink any water that day. He realized that he hadn't and that he hadn't seen her eat at all either. "Hey, Naomi, did you notice if Mona ate or drank anything, anything at all, today or yesterday?"

"Not sure... fuck. I don't think she did you know?"

They sterilized some water and poured a few drops down her throat, then a few more. Jasper knew it was his fault, he'd been pushing way, way too hard. Well, what could have been solved in a few short rests was now a life threatening situation that might take days to resolve. He'd been avoiding reaching out to the voice on the other end of the walkie talkie - he didn't know anything about them other than that they seemed organized and were making regular runs. At this point, it needed to happen.

He took the walkie talkie and flipped the talk button. "Hi, my Name is Jasper Pellerine. I'm not sure of my exact location, but there are three of us, and one of us is incapacitated. We are extremely low on food. If there is anyone there, please help." Then he waited.

The wait seemed like forever, but eventually, a strong voice came on the line, "Hi Jasper. My name's Robert. I'm coming to you... can you give me an approximate location?"

Naomi took over the phone. "Hi, Robert, Naomi here. We are at forty-five point one three lat, minus 62 point nine eight long, or close to. Sorry, that's the best I can do, no GPS, can't see no stars. Shit's hard to figure right now."

Jasper knew she was good with directions, but to be able to give that level of detail without equipment was still surprising. Jasper sat down to wait, exhausted, but Naomi said "Come on motherfucker. Too much shit to do, you heard? Light a fire. Give the man a chance to actually find us, I'm good at this shit, but I'm probably off by a bit. Ain't no zombies coming to check out smoke anyway. Get your ass UP!"

He set to work. Another surprise, and another underestimation. Here he was playing leader, playing the big survivor, and here he was putting other people's lives in needless danger, while a slip of a girl and a meth head were keeping him alive with their talents and intelligence. He needed to re-think the way he thought about people. He realized he'd been dismissing them because they were women, and in his head he had it fixed that men are the survivors, the strong ones.

They kept a damp cloth on Mona's forehead. After a little while, her breathing started to get deeper and her pulse slowed. She opened her eyes and tried to get up.

"Stay there, we have people coming to help. You passed out from dehydration, probably hunger too. Just lie there and get your strength back," Jasper said.

"K."

Finally, two men came out of the woods, wearing camouflage clothing, carrying heavy backpacks, small crossbows in hand. They each had a rifle slung over their shoulder as well.

The two of them looked nothing alike, one was white, with blonde hair. The other one was black with a shaved head. Despite that, they seemed the same somehow. It was the way they carried themselves, the way they dressed, the equipment they carried. The blonde one said, "Hey, you Jasper? I'm Robert. Nice to meet you."

"Yeah, I'm Jasper. This is Naomi, and the one lying down is Mona. She's in pretty rough shape. Guess I forgot that the human body needs fuel. Been pushing us way too hard for a bit now."

"Okay. Naomi, the human GPS. Nice to meet you as well. This is Tom. He's our medic, he'll look over your friend."

Tom checked Mona over, and then pulled out an IV bag from his pack and hung it from a tree, before poking a needle into Mona's arm. He had some trouble finding a vein, taking his time, getting her to flex as much as she could, but he managed it after a few minutes.

Robert sat down by the fire on a little folding stool he carried. He offered Jasper and Naomi some beef jerky.

"What brings you folks to this part of the province?" asked Robert. His tone was casual, but there was an edge to it.

"We're heading to Charlottetown. My kid is there."

"Okay, that makes sense. I was actually planning on hitting PEI as well. Good farmland."

"You guys military?"

"I am. Tom's reserves. The group of us are a bit mixed, but mostly either active or ex. We had a plan starting before this hit. Fucking zombies. It was a joke right? Like, we had a plan for if shit went fucked up, called it the zombie plan, but none of us figured that would actually happen. Well, guess the jokes on us."

"Yeah, I did a bunch of survival training. Used to tell my ex it was for the zombies. I was kidding. So far it's been pretty damned useful."

"Shit... Jasper Pellerine. You took the wilderness survival stuff at Canada Survival School a few years back didn't you?."

"Wait, that was you? This place man, it's like a small town of half a million. Yeah, I remember you. Big Rob the superstar student. I remember you got that fire going in the middle of the rain storm. Damn, good to see you."

Jasper hadn't liked Robert all that much during training, but he seemed to be the only one. Everyone else was grateful to the big man who could make fire under any circumstances, could make a shelter in half the time the rest of them took, managed to get a dozen fish when the rest of them couldn't get a single one. Jasper knew that he tended to be a judgmental prick and that just the fact that someone owned a hockey jersey unfairly prejudiced him against them. Not to mention

Robert clearly had a competent group with lots of supplies and lots of food. The fact that he was headed to PEI was a major bonus. Screw prejudice, better to go with them and survive to find his little girl.

After a while, Tom gave the all clear for Mona to move. Robert told them that he was set up just outside of Upper Musquodoboit, a small town a little to the north. They walked for a couple of hours, moving slowly to accommodate Mona's condition. Roberts camp was invisible until they were standing almost inside it. There were tents, a dozen small ones and a few large ones, covered in branches and leaves. The whole thing was in a depression in the ground, which made Jasper nervous until he noticed a wide swale that would let water drain out, preventing flooding.

The camp was tidy and industrious. It was also very, very quiet. Somehow the group of people there seemed to be able to work in almost perfect silence. There were other defences once you got close. Ditches filled with spikes pointing out. Pits covered in dirt that were almost invisible until you were on top of them. Snipers in trees that could only be seen once you were on the other side of them. That probably meant more that were simply invisible unless you were right on top of them.

Robert brought them into one of the large tents. A mess hall. The inside was lined with some sort of silver material. "Sound dampening, we can talk in here, still not too loud," he answered when Mona pointed it out.

There was a makeshift counter with trays and food containers. "Grab a bite," Robert said, "It's edible, barely."

They grabbed trays, thankful to finally have something to eat. The food selection was limited. Scrambled eggs, some bacon, pancakes. A breakfast spread despite it being nearly supper time at this point. They wolfed down the food as Robert sat there and waited. Finally, when they were done he got to the point. "Look, everything I have given you so far is free of charge. However, we don't carry dead weight here.

If you want to join us, you have to contribute. You are welcome, hell, there's not enough living humans around for us to turn away able bodies, but you have to carry your own weight and you have to follow the rules. The rules are strict, but they aren't arbitrary. Follow orders. No conversation in the open. We scavenge empty places. Anything scavenged goes into the communal pot. Everything. No gunfire obviously, it draws them. We have crossbows. I notice you have traditional bows. That's all good, you keep those. The dog. Does he bark?"

"Nope," Jasper said, "He's only barked once to let me know there was one about to get me. He's figured out how to take down a zombie and keep away from the dangerous bits."

"Alright. He's welcome too. Just like you though, has to pull his weight. Other than that, we don't usually stay in one place very long. You folks clearly have been sharing a tent. That seems like a reasonable arrangement for now. You will get watch duty. Clearly, Mona needs a day or two before she's going to be able to do her turn".

"I'm tough, used to not sleeping. Can keep watch now."

Robert chuckled. "No, I think we give you a day or so. Not worried about you being tough enough, just don't to waste all that nice saline fluid Tom dropped in your veins."

They got squared away and then one of the other soldiers showed Jasper where he would be set up for watch. The camp seemed to be about ninety percent male, and there seemed to be a lot more people than the number of tents would indicate.

There was also a low wooden platform in the middle of the camp. It didn't seem to fit. A round platform of wood that was large enough to fit about ten people if they were tightly packed. It was on legs that were less than a foot tall. The whole thing might have stood a foot and a half above the ground. Everything else had a clear purpose, but the platform was just there.

Watch was uneventful but hard. The camp was doing three hour watches, and staying awake for three hours starting at two o'clock in the morning was a challenge after pushing so hard for so long. The camp had a few pairs of night vision goggles, and Jasper was issued a set for his watch. The landscape was converted into a series of greens and blacks, but the goggles made it clear and easy to see. When he was relieved he was still awake and alert. The first light had started to appear on the horizon, just a faint glimmer.

Jasper lay down in the tent and slept instantly.

Halfway between the north pole and the equator

Jasper had only been in bed for an hour when Naomi shook him awake. Breakfast was first, then Robert wanted to address the group. Apparently, Jasper, Naomi, and Mona were the third group to get to eat. The food was identical to supper, but there was a lot of it and no rationing. After they had finished Robert cleared his throat and started speaking. His voice carried through the room, even though he was barely talking above a whisper.

"Okay, we've taken as much as we can from Upper Musquodoboit. The place is pretty overrun and we can't risk moving in. It's time to get going. I know travel is a bitch these days, but it's time to pack up and hit the road. Work details are posted on the main board at the back of this tent. Eat up, then get to work."

He walked out, not pausing to see the reaction to his announcement. A bunch of the men groaned, but Jasper was happy, every delay made him panic a little bit inside. His main concern with joining Robert's band was that it would slow him down too much. If it kept him alive though, arriving was better than not.

The teardown of the camp was quick and efficient. By ten in the morning, they were ready to get on the road. Jasper was assigned to tearing down the mess hall with Naomi, while Mona was excused for the day. Nobody seemed to begrudge her. Most people didn't realize that she had looked that thin before the zombies appeared and assumed it was evidence she was frail and failing.

Life with the group was vastly different from the nomadic life that the trio had suffered prior to meeting the group. Everything was structured. Breaks came at regular intervals, with watches set. As Naomi was working with Jasper she got to chatting with one of the other women in the camp. "You look familiar, where have I seen you before?" the woman said.

"You ever eat at the Caribbean place in the north end?"

"Yeah, that's it. You worked behind the counter right?"

"Yep. That me. Didn't think anything would make me miss the work, but yeah... I'd go back in a minute."

"You do any of the cooking there or just serve?"

"Auntie was teaching me to make it all. I always helped."

"We have to get you in the kitchen, maybe you can make some of this slop taste like actual food."

The woman dragged Naomi away to talk to the cook, leaving Jasper with most of the manual labour.

The next day Jasper got assigned scouting duty. He took Snow with him, both of them eager to be useful, and in Jasper's case especially to be moving the group ahead faster. They took off each morning, running quietly. Jasper could run far more than five kilometres these days. Any fat he had had on his body had melted away on the journey, and his stride, developed over months of running, was longer, surer. His skin was dark from weeks spent in the open. He looked like a pre-apocalypse homeless man, hair dirty and tousled, clothing ragged, layered. They bathed as often as they could, but even in the camp, it wasn't often. Despite the amount of water in the area they had to carry what they used.

Snow would range ahead and to each side, sniffing the air for signs of zombies. If he found them he would come back to Jasper, silently letting his master know something dangerous was ahead. The two of them were the most effective scouting party in the group, the dog's sense of smell put them ahead of any of the exclusively human groups.

At night Jasper would come back to camp, hang out with Mona and Naomi if they were available. Mona was given nothing but light duty, so she was always available. Naomi was in the mess tent most of the time, and the food was better. She always hung out with Jasper and Mona after shift though.

"Why don't you ever hang with the soldiers?"

"They grab my ass too much. These boys got no manners. You look at my tits, I notice it, but I don't mind. You never grab me or nothing. I like you."

"Alright, duly noted. I'll be more careful with my gaze in the future." Jasper was thrown by Naomi's very frank manner.

"Nah, it's all good. Not like I don't look at pretty boys. You feel free to look."

Things were easier. Robert kept paying special attention to the three of them. He made excuses to visit their tent every evening, made sure his meals corresponded with theirs. Then one night Mona spent the night in the command tent and the reason clear. From that point on Robert and Mona were together.

Jasper felt his frustration with the pace mounting. They were moving as fast as possible, but a group that size with gear and no vehicles doesn't move fast. He needed to stay alive to reach Charlottetown, and his odds were much better if he was with the group, so he managed to put it aside, day after slowly moving day.

Jasper was heading back from scouting duty and found the camp, except the active duty watches, clustered around the wooden platform. Robert was standing in the centre of the platform, another piece of wood was slotted into a groove, forming a pillar. One of the men was handcuffed to the pillar, naked to the waist.

"This man slept on watch, endangering all of us," Robert said, "I will not tolerate chaos and disorder in this camp. You have jobs to do, and when one of you doesn't do it we are all at risk. Imagine if his negligence had caused a breach, imagine if you, or your wife, or your child, had been killed because of him."

He took out a heavy leather whip and laid into the man. The whole thing was done in silence. The soldier had a gag in his mouth, preventing him from screaming or crying out. His body jerked with every stroke. He tried to scream around the gag, but it rendered him mute. After a half dozen precise strokes Robert stopped.

Jasper was sickened. He understood the purpose, he just didn't think it was effective. If it kept this sort of incident from occurring maybe it was justified, but Jasper was pretty sure it didn't - the man fell asleep because he was run to the edge of his endurance, not because he was lazy or shiftless. Jasper had seen this sort of thing from Robert when they were on course together. Robert was a bully. He was larger than most people and used his size to intimidate. It was often subtle, standing too close to someone, invading their space. On the course, he had lost his temper once, and only once, but it had been with a smaller woman who was having a hard time starting a fire. He screamed at her until she broke down in tears, then he walked away. Everyone had attributed it to the stress at the time, however, Jasper was seeing a pattern emerge.

They started to run low on supplies after a few weeks, right when they were reaching Middle Stewiacke, a small town with a few restaurants and a co-op grocery store. The plan was simple. Move in under cover of darkness in small teams, most of them assigned to draw the zombies, two other teams to raid the grocery store. Jasper and Snow pulled decoy duty. Naomi and Mona were sitting this one out. Robert deemed Naomi's other duties too important to risk her, and Mona was never required to work anymore.

The walk into town was tense. They were part of a team of five, Snow made six, but only Jasper counted him. The rest of the team was mixed. There were two women, Candice and Sasha, and two men, Matt and Jordan. Sasha was an older woman with grey hair and a permanent scowl. Candice was young and fit. Jasper pegged her as white trash. Matt was a young private, and Jordan might have been Matt's twin. The six of them moved into town, splitting from the other groups right away. They wandered for a few minutes, making noise, yelling, hitting things. They started to attract a lot of attention, groups of zombies forming up behind them.

After about fifteen minutes the primary groups sent off two flares, the signal that they had reached their target. Jasper and company took a prearranged route out of town. The way had been prepped in advance, they studied all the possible routes to their destination.

They started moving faster. So far they'd been keeping pace with the zombies, making sure to stay close, to get as many following as possible. Now they needed to be a bit ahead of them, to give themselves a tiny bit of breathing room, while not losing the horde.

Ahead of them the mouth of the alleyway yawned, dark and foreboding. Even in the light of day, it was dark and hard to see, a narrow gap between low buildings. They ran for it, a couple of hundred zombies behind them. There was the ramp, as promised, leading up a short wall - only about eight feet. The group ran up the ramp, Jasper in the lead. The zombies followed, close behind. Matt kicked the ramp down as he went over. Snow wasn't all the way up yet, front paws still inches from safety. He jumped as the board fell, barely clearing the wall. The rest of them climbed up a fire escape that almost touched the short wall. They dropped the iron stairs, giving Snow an opportunity to climb up. As soon as he was sure Snow was safe, Jasper punched Matt in the jaw. He knocked the soldier down with one shot, then lifted him up and held him over the edge of the fire escape. "You don't risk his life. Got it? You don't fucking risk his life."

Matt was crying, bawling with fear. If Jasper dropped him he would fall into the horde below, and from the look on his face, he knew it "please, please, I'm sorry. Please, let me up."

Jasper didn't care about Matt's tears. Snow was visibly limping, he'd hurt his leg in the leap. Jasper was pretty sure it wasn't broken, but not one hundred percent. He was seeing red, wanting to drop the soldier into waiting horde. Jordan and Candice were trying to pull Matt back up, grabbing the fabric of his pants, keeping him steady. Sasha, on the other hand, didn't seem to care. She pulled a crumpled pack of cigarettes from her jacket and lit one, taking a long drag. Finally, Jasper pulled Matt up and let him drop to the landing. He kneed the soldier in the face. Matt dropped prone, nose broken.

"Alright, time to get to it. We have a schedule to keep."

He started up the fire escape. It was a set of steel stairs. This time he made sure Snow was right behind him. Matt was moving slowly behind the group, hanging back. He was silent. They made it up to the roof and dropped the gate on the other side of the alley. They had several hundred zombies trapped in the narrow space.

They headed out. Matt trailing slowly. There were still a few zombies on the street, only small numbers, easily dealt with. Snow was still favouring his right front leg. Once they got out of town Matt called out. "Jasper, wait."

Jasper stopped to wait. He knew he could take Matt, especially now that the man was injured.

"Look, I'm sorry. I didn't think," Matt said, "I was panicked. I understand why you went after me. You were right. My nose fucking hurts, but I earned it."

"Alright. Apology accepted."

"We good?"

"Yeah. We're good. Don't let it happen again."

They caught up to the group, Matt moving at full speed now.

"Look, guys, let me deal with the nose thing. It was my fuckup, I don't want Robert knowing the details. Just let me take my lumps. Anyone asks, I fell jumping to the fire escape, banged my face. It's a dangerous job right?" he said with a pained wink.

Jasper was surprised. He found he had gained respect for the soldier, his willingness to accept fault, his understanding of what Jasper had done. They headed back to camp.

The run was a success. They did lose two but managed to get enough food for several weeks. Robert was in a dark mood, however, as a result of the death of the two men.

Everything falls apart in the end

Eventually, food ran low again. By this point, they were near Truro. Truro was much larger than Stewiacke, a medium sized town with some suburbs, a central hub in the province. Jasper didn't like the idea of using the same tactics here as they had been in the past. A larger town meant a lot more zombies. Different places should mean different tactics. Jasper took Robert aside, "Look, man, there's way too many for the Stewiacke plan to work. We're going to get pinned down, cut off, it's too many."

"It will work. You've only seen this a couple of times. We have done it a shitload of times." Robert was playing with his baton as he talked, extending it, collapsing it, extending it again.

"Let's figure something else out, a better way to do this. We need to evaluate based on the conditions on the ground."

"Maybe I've been unclear, too nice or something. You are a nice guy, but you are a civilian. This is a military operation. As soon as you joined up you joined the army. Either you follow orders or you take a turn on the platform. Up to you, makes no difference to me either way."

Jasper ended up deciding to go ahead with the plan, but to make sure he had an exit, alternate ways out of town even if they didn't help with the mission. The setup was the same as last time, lure zombies into blind alleys, into traps. Cut them off, then take the supplies. The plan started pretty much the same, moving around, getting a crowd following them. It took Jasper a few minutes to be clear that things were not going smoothly. The numbers were larger, much larger. In fact, they were even larger than expected with the increased population. Somewhere along the line a bunch of extra zombies had shown up in Truro.

They started heading to the pre-arranged alleyway but kept finding themselves cut off. Every turn they made, there were hordes of zombies ahead of them. The six of them had learned to move well together, and Jasper kept them moving despite the route being cut off. He kept looking for an angle, for some way to get out of there. The horde was close when they hit downtown. They made it to the core of the old town, surrounded by ancient buildings, Jasper taking them on one of his planned escape routes. There was a department store, a relic of a bygone era. Jasper had been in there once years earlier with Karen, it would do the trick, at least if his memory was correct. From the exterior, it appeared to be a series of buildings, but inside it all connected. Not only that, the levels connected in weird ways. Jasper kicked the door at one end of the store open. The rest of the group had no idea why this place, but they followed. "Hope you have a plan dude. Not keen on getting eaten," Jordan said as he ducked inside the ancient building.

"Just wait, this place will work for us."

"K, trusting you dude."

The first building was a single level, but there was a stairway down just inside the arch to the next building, so Jasper took it. They knocked over clothing racks as they went. The basement had more clothing, and they tore through it, crossing three more surface structures, knocking down racks behind them, anything to slow the zombies. Finally, Jasper led them up in the farthest one of the group. There was a narrow staircase leading up from there, and it had a door. The door was solid wood, enough to last at least a few minutes. Jasper pulled it shut behind them, right behind Snow. They ran up to the top retail floor. There was another door here, this one with an employees only sign on it. Unfortunately one of the employees was there already, and long dead. Snow wrapped his teeth around the zombie's arm, pulling him to the floor and Matt spiked his head. They headed up that flight of stairs into an office area. He found what he was looking for, a rear facing fire escape, and then set all of the papers in the manager's office on fire. The place lit up fast as the team climbed out the window and down.

The streets were still crawling with zombies, but the fire seemed to be drawing a lot of them. The group headed out of town as fast as they could. They made it out and into the surrounding woods, unobserved by the crowds of undead wandering the streets.

Travel was ridiculously slow. They had to make it several kilometres through woodland, with zombies wandering everywhere. The area around Truro was thick with them, the team was still getting cut off, still having to backtrack every few minutes. They ended up getting caught by small clusters twice and had to fight their way free. It was touch and go, One of the zombies bit through Sasha's uniform, but missed her skin.

Finally, they made it back to base camp. There was a skeleton crew still there. Robert and Mona were sitting in the mess tent, Naomi was in the kitchen trying to make something for the returning soldiers, not knowing they were already mostly dead, and a few others were scattered around. Jasper came in, strode straight to Robert and punched him. Robert fell on his back, but rolled back to his feet without pausing, "What the fuck?"

"I told you. Too many, far, far too many. They cut us off, the plan didn't stand a chance."

"You made it back, you left your unit, and you came back? You fucking chickenshit. That's desertion."

"Fuck you! The plan failed. All of them are dead. We should be dead."

Matt, Jordan, Candice, and Sasha were standing behind Jasper, visibly lending him the weight of their support. Something had changed when Jasper got them out of Truro alive, they were with him. Naomi came out from behind the kitchen area and stood with them as well.

Robert pulled a gun. They didn't typically use guns, the noise drew zombies, so Jasper had completely forgotten about them. Clearly, Robert hadn't. "No, fuck you. We suffered a loss. We keep going. We fight on. You are a chickenshit little bitch. Knew I shouldn't have let a civilian in. Now, get down on your knees."

Robert had the advantage. Nobody else had a gun on them. Jasper went to his knees. Robert threw him a pair of cuffs and told him to put them on. A bunch of Roberts men came in to check out the commotion. Robert pointed at Jasper and his group, "Arrest them".

The newcomers snapped to it, grabbing the six of them. That was a problem. When one of them tried to grab Jasper Snow grabbed him, shaking the man with his powerful jaws, pulling him to the ground. Robert kicked the big dog in the ribs, sending him to the ground. Snow tried to leap at him, Robert levelled his gun at the big dog's head. He fired, catching Snow between the eyes. Jasper gasped, something broke inside him, leaving him more animal than human. He jumped to his feet and rushed Robert, slamming his body into the larger man. He had the cuffs on his right wrist, but the soldiers hadn't put them on the left yet. He started smashing Robert in the face with his right hand, the left cuff wrapped around it. He hit again, and again, and again. His vision was pure red, anger taking over completely. He felt arms wrapping around him, pulling him back. He was driven to the ground, the weight of three people on his back. He felt a hard impact to the side of his head and everything went black.

When the lights came back on for Jasper he was on his knees, hands bound and attached to the ground. He was on the wooden platform in the middle of the camp, leather gag in his mouth. He could see the rest of his group by the platform, hands and ankles bound. Snow's corpse was also there, blood running through his white fur, eyes open and fixed. The few other surviving soldiers were watching, not really enough to form a crowd. Of the more than fifty soldiers that started the day out, there were only fifteen now, including Jasper and the other prisoners.

Jasper felt the leather whip hit his back. The pain was more than he could imagine. He felt his flesh part. The whip came down again. He screamed, as loud as he could. The gag prevented him from making a noise. The heavy piece of leather kept coming. He lost count after seven strokes, consciousness after twelve.

He woke up to water being splashed in his face. Robert was standing over him as he lay on the ground, fists balled at his sides, face full of anger. The men pulled him up and pushed him to the side. They pulled Jordan out next, stripped him to the waist and put him on the post. He got a total of five lashes, then they moved on. Each one was stripped to the waist and tied to the pole. Naomi was last. Robert had a strange light in his eyes. He didn't stop at stripping her to the waist, instead stripping her naked and chaining her up. As he pulled her clothes off she stood, chin up, showing no hint of shame or embarrassment. When he finally got her stripped she looked him in the eye and spat. He backhanded her across the face and pushed the gag between her teeth. He pushed her slender naked body into a kneeling position in front of the post and chained her in place. The whole time she stayed rigid, forcing him to use his strength, to exert himself. She knew she wasn't strong enough to stop him, but she didn't give him a single inch. He whipped her, and her body shrugged with the blow, but she didn't cry out. It wasn't until the third lash that she tried to scream. He gave her eight. Afterwards, she stood and looked him in the eye, then she went over to Jasper and put her arms around him, soothing him as he lay on the ground sobbing.

Escape

That night none of them could move. They were all in too much pain, bodies broken, spirits damaged or destroyed. Robert had set one tent aside with two cages in it, apparently foreseeing that he would have to lock people up.

Jasper was losing it. Snow was what had kept him together so far. The idea of Taylor of course, but Snow's solid presence at his side, the reliability of the big dog, the absolute loyalty, that got him through the day to day, kept him fighting when every part of him wanted to give up. He knew that he needed to get it together, to start figuring out how to get the hell out of there. He was sure Robert was going to kill him, probably as soon as he could manage to justify it, but he just didn't have enough left in him to do what he needed to do. He was tapped.

The six of them were separated by gender, women in one cage, men in the other. Their clothing hadn't been returned to them, and their shoes were taken when they were put in the cages. All of them except Naomi were shirtless. She was completely naked. Jasper felt more vulnerable than he ever had in his life. Naomi seemed defiant, angry instead of ashamed.

Matt was the one who gave them a chance at escape. He didn't even mean to. He collapsed from the pain, crying out as he did so. The guard said, "Shut up. You want to bring the zombies? Shut the fuck up".

"He can't," Jordan said, "He needs some water and some pain killers. You want him to shut up you give him what he needs".

"Fuck. Alright. Just shut his damned mouth."

The guard came over, pushing a glass of water through the bars. Jasper snapped. He wasn't trying to escape, he needed to hurt someone. He grabbed the guard's arm and broke it with a single quick movement. Realizing what he had just done, he said, "Give me the fucking keys. You think this hurts now? I can make it worse."

"let go. Please. Here." The guard handed him the keys. Jasper handed them to Jordan, keeping a firm grip on the guard. After the cage was open Jordan smashed the guard in the side of the head. The guard dropped, stunned. Jordan walked the two steps to the women's cage and let them out as well. They got Matt up. He stopped moaning, forcing himself to get it together.

Jasper was running on autopilot. If it weren't for Taylor he would have gone back and killed Robert. He still had a faint hope that Taylor was alive, that despite all the delays, despite the odds that she had died on the first night, she was still there, waiting for him. It wasn't much, but it was enough.

Naomi took over the leadership position. She started making decisions, not waiting for anyone else. Everyone went along, they were too broken to decide for themselves. Jasper was relieved, the burden off of his shoulders. Naomi slit open the fabric tent just above the ground and snuck underneath the back edge, looking around. Nobody was watching. It was full dark and the sky was heavily overcast, so it was nearly impossible to see.

They snuck through the camp, moving on hands and knees, crawling with their bellies to the ground. Sharp grasses poked at them, piercing bare flesh, a thousand tiny spikes.

They were in a small wooded area, a few acres at most. Most of the area was farmland, another reason Jasper had been so strongly opposed to Robert's plan. While the town would have netted the greatest cache the surrounding farms all would have stores, some even surviving livestock. The raid hadn't been needed.

They snuck through the woods to the nearest farm. It was hard to keep quiet, all of them had massive lacerations on their backs, being pulled open by their crawling movements. The wounds had barely started to scab over, so each step pulled the scabs loose, leaving blood dripping down their ribs. Each step forward filled them with pain, a fresh need to cry out.

They could barely make out the silhouette of the large farmhouse, a faintly darker black against the clouds. They made their way, all of them missing shirts and shoes, Naomi fully naked. With no light, they were always stepping on thorns or rocks. All of them moved slowly, painfully, towards the house. When they finally made it to the door the sun was just starting to lighten the horizon. They could make out a giant barn, many fields, a variety of farm equipment.

The door was shut, but when Jasper tried the knob it turned and the door swung out towards them. They heard shuffling and groaning from inside. With weapons and gear, individual zombies were not much threat. Without boots, let alone a knife, a single zombie in the dark was potentially deadly. If a single one of them was bitten it would be devastating. They were so few, they needed each other. With all they had just lost Jasper didn't think he could bear to lose anyone else.

Jasper slammed the door shut. The zombie inside hadn't reached the doorway, and Jasper made sure the door shut firmly. They looked around the porch for anything they could use as a weapon, but whoever had lived here had kept the place exceptionally tidy. There was a small shed close by. It was locked, so Matt grabbed a rock from the ground and smashed the padlock open with a single blow.

Inside they found a few gardening implements, this wasn't where the farming tools were kept. Just simple tools for maintaining the neat patch of flowers in front of the house. Jasper took the edger, Matt took the long spade shaped shovel. The rest of the tools were small, and not useful. There were a few poles against one wall. Candice and Sasha took those. Naomi grabbed the gardening apron hanging on one wall and put that on.

They headed back to the porch and positioned themselves at the ready. Naomi opened the door and stayed behind it while the others waited, makeshift weapons poised to strike. The zombie lurched out, followed by another, and then two more. Small ones. Looked like the entire family had turned inside. Sasha moved in and pressed the pole against one of the children and Candice did the same with the other. Jasper slammed the edger into the male's throat. He pushed, dropping his weight into the creature. The creature fell back into the wall. Jasper kept leaning his weight forward as the zombie reached for him, hands grabbing at flesh made slippery with blood. Finally, the edger hit wood on the far side of the creature's neck. Its head fell off and it dropped to the ground.

Matt swung his shovel at the woman. He caught her low, hitting her on the shoulder. She got one hand around him and started pulling herself toward him, teeth gnashing. Jordan grabbed her and pulled her back. Jasper came in and slammed the creature in the side of the head. She dropped, fluid leaking from her temple.

The kids only took a moment. Jasper hated it when he had to deal with child zombies, but it was slowly starting to bother him less. He wasn't sure he was okay with that. Killing children should bother him, even if they are already dead.

They went into the house, cautious but fairly confident. It was getting light out bit by bit and at this point, they could see fairly well. The entry was open to the interior of the house. It had a simple wooden bench, with tole painted ducks on it. There were boots next to the bench and jackets hung up above it. Past the foyer, they found a living room. It had a well-stuffed couch and chair, a lay-z-boy. There was a very large television on the wall.

Jordan was the one that noticed a light on the TV. Just a small red standby light. It meant that there was power in the house though, somehow. They found the remote on the TV and hit power. The TV came on to static. They kept flipping channels until finally, they found one that was broadcasting. It was nothing but a text screen on coloured bars, the emergency broadcast system. It was also making a horrible noise, but they hit mute.

"It appears that the dead have come back to life. They are atempting to murder and consum the living. If you see one of these creatures destroy the creatures brain or cut its head off. No other injuries will do the job".

The language of the message was informal and brief. It didn't make a whole lot of sense and didn't give them any other information. It contained spelling and grammatical mistakes. It was the closest to anything official any of them had seen.

"Well, fuck," Matt said, "The world really has gone to hell."

"Not like we thought it would be different," Naomi said as she grabbed a pair of shoes from the bench. The shoes were her size. That left Sasha and Candice out of luck, both had larger feet than Naomi. Naomi managed to find some other clothes as well. They were all much, much too large for her. She didn't care, it was better than being naked. All of them managed to find shirts that worked, even if they were far too large. The guys all had smaller feet than the farmer, but with extra pairs of socks, they were okay.

They spread out to search the house. Jordan called out from the back room, "Guys, come quick... we have guns here. Farmer John was a hunter."

Next to the guns, there was a bunch of cold weather gear, a pair of short range talkies, and two large packs. The kitchen was stocked, and the fridge was full of food, still running. Civilization, even if they couldn't stay for long. "This is the shit." Naomi said "We need this. Let's take a minute, get rested up, hit the road tomorrow."

Jasper didn't have the heart to answer. He dropped on the couch, the pain in his back when he sat down was almost enough to knock him out, he let out a low grunt, then turned over onto his stomach, passing out almost instantly. The group spent the day recovering. They all took hot showers, took naps, relaxed for the day. It was needed. There was also a decently stocked medicine cabinet. They spread antibiotic cream over the whip marks, bound their wounds properly, healed, and rested.

That night they spent in the house. They made sure not to use lights that were visible to the outside. There was even a spare room and a fold out couch in the living room. In the end, each of them had a bed to themselves. They hauled the bodies out of sight and locked everything up. Jasper was sure they should have set a watch, but with all the pain and loss of the last day he couldn't work up the energy to suggest it.

The next morning they explored the farm, looking for anything they might use. Progress was slow, none of them could move fast. There was a giant barn. They opened the door... the stench was unbelievable. The cows had been without food since the zombies appeared, and whether it was that or disease spreading through them, they were all dead. Had been for a while. The barn was hot, and the smell of rotten meat was thick in the air. The corpses of the cows were covered in flies, their flesh writhed with maggots. The smells of cow shit and sour milk were there underlying the rotten meat.

They shut the door on the barn. Naomi said, "Winter gonna be bad. What the fuck are people going to eat?"

Nobody had an answer for her.

They headed to the garage. There was a large truck inside, a jacked up hot wheels toy with an extended cab, full of gas. They knew that the vehicle was going to attract zombies, but decided it was worth the risk to get ahead of Robert and his people. The truck roared to life and they headed out. The flatbed full of food and supplies.

Sasha took the wheel, the most experienced driver of the bunch. "Which way boss lady?"

"Take the highway. No way we going through town. Sides, I don't know shit about Truro. Ain't never been before. Too many fucking zombies."

They hit the highway going fast. They were easily doing a hundred and sixty by the time they made the town. There were a few cars, but the highway was nice and wide by that point. They managed not to hit any of them. There was also a couple of zombies, Sasha kept her foot on the gas and the hood aimed right at them. They went right through the zombies like they weren't there.

The exit they wanted, the one leading west to New Brunswick, had an overturned semi-truck on it. The truck had crashed into the support pillar, and the entire highway in that direction was hanging on by a thread. Jasper had done a course in Tatamagouche a few years back during the winter, and he had taken the back roads to it, so he vaguely remembered the route. It would get them to PEI eventually. They hit the other exit and moved off the one oh two onto the one oh four, going east instead of west.

The road was decent going this way. Nobody seemed to have been fleeing towards Cape Breton. One or two derelict cars, otherwise their route was clear for the time being.

Chase

Robert was furious. He had trusted them, let them into his camp, against his better judgement. Should have kept the numbers tight. Now, two of the three were gone, and with them a bunch of his men. The worst part was that they had left things in chaos. Their escape left him with an injured man and a bunch of questions that he didn't have answers for.

Jasper would have to pay, of course. He was going to need to be made an example of or else discipline would slip among the men. The others could be allowed back in after sufficient punishment. Naomi could also be allowed to live. She was a good cook, and now that he knew her true colours he would use her as entertainment for the men between her regular duties. The slut didn't deserve anything else. He kept thinking about the curve of her ass as she was kneeling down on the post, the way her hips moved as he brought the whip down on her back. Every time he pictured it he got hard. He usually went and found Mona in those moments. At least she had proved to be loyal, to be his. Sure, she wasn't that hot, but it was the fucking apocalypse, and she wasn't ugly. Just bad teeth and a bit too skinny.

He rounded up his few remaining men. How the hell had Truro gone so wrong? They used the same tactic in every town, and it always worked. Jasper again. He had screwed up the plan somehow. Him and that fucking dog. Well, at least he had something out of it, a nice new fur. He skinned the damn thing. He was going to tan it, wear it around his shoulders when it started to get cold.

It took most of the day to get started with so few of them left. They had to secure the camp, make sure they were ready to move. Of course, they had to leave most of the equipment behind, they didn't have the manpower to carry it anymore. Then they had to track the escapees from the back of the prison tent. They lost them a few times, the ground around the camp was so heavily trampled. By the time they were on Jaspers trail it was more than twenty-four hours since he had escaped.

They reached a farm that the prisoners had obviously fled to and saw the bodies on the porch. Robert heard an engine start up somewhere nearby. He ran as fast as he could and saw the truck as it sped out of sight. He knew the group had escaped, at least for the time being. Time to make the most of it and use the farm for himself and his loyal men, give them a reward for their service.

They moved the camp to the farm over the next day, and Robert used the main house for himself. Mona stayed with him. There was very little food, of course, he assumed Jasper and his group had taken it, but it turned out there was a root cellar that was still well stocked. Guess they missed that, typical, anything Jasper touched was going to be half assed. How the hell had he not seen it in the man? Jasper was careless. Of course, the barn was unusable, or else they could have had fresh beef as well.

Staying in the house for a few days seemed like the only logical course of action. He needed to decompress, and the men needed some time to recover. He knew where Jasper was headed, and he was pretty sure he could get there much faster when it came down to it. He was smarter, better trained, better equipped. He would make them pay for their insubordination.

The men were quiet, very subdued. Of course they were, they had suffered a major loss. Robert made sure they had good food, mostly out of the root cellar. He sent a couple of them scouting, and they found chickens at the next farm. The chickens were very skinny, but still alive, and there were a lot of them. It wasn't a real farm, not like this one. Just a place some hippies clearly put together. The chickens were in a very large pen and had been scrounging. He had a few of them killed and put together a small feast.

Three days. He gave himself three days and then he hit the road. They were on foot of course, but he was giving some thought to finding horses. They were quieter, maybe they wouldn't attract zombies the same way a car running did. They also had the ability to fuel themselves if there was grass, and you could eat them if needed.

They kept moving from farm to farm. There were people on most of them, but they were already dead so they didn't mind when he took over. He eventually found a farm with horses. He was already an experienced rider, and most of his men caught on quickly. Sure, it delayed them a couple of days to get everyone up to practice. Mona had a hard time with it, but in the end, she was good enough. At first, she wasn't really trying, but a bit of attitude correction on his part and she got better at it. He did feel bad though. Her teeth really were pretty bad, still, he didn't mean to knock one of them out.

Abandoned

The group was moving fast, faster than they had since the world ended. They got a few kilometres on the highway, then had to take smaller roads. Even so, this was passthrough country, no real towns, a few houses by the side of the road with a sign saying "Welcome to..." and then more empty countryside.

The radio in the truck wasn't picking up anything so they drove in silence. In about an hour they made it further than they would have over the course of a week on foot. They arrived at a spot where the only way forward was across a bridge. One of the support pillars was half collapsed, and the deck was listing heavily to one side. "What you guys think, should we risk it?" Sasha said.

"Fuck no. You crazy? That ain't holdin this truck. Don't know bout you, but I don't feel like swimming right now."

They climbed out of the truck and got as much of the contents as they could on their bodies. They had to leave some of it behind, so they sat down and had a picnic before braving the structure.

Matt took on the job of distributing the gear, filling the packs and handing them to people. Jasper noticed that Naomi ended up with mostly lighter things. He didn't think she realized it.

Jasper hung on to the railing of the bridge as he went, feeling every moment like he was going to fall off. It wasn't a big drop, only twenty feet or so, but the bridge was shaking underfoot, and every breeze felt like it was going to take the whole thing out. Over the worst section, he was using his arms to hold himself on, his feet struggling to find purchase. Naomi had sweat dripping down her face, and Jasper could see the strain in her arms. She was visibly trembling with effort.

Finally, they reached the far shore, back on solid ground. Naomi collapsed from the strain, gasping for air. She was drenched. "Guys, I'm good. Just give me two minutes, I be back on my feet."

She was true to her word, after two minutes she stood up, still looking green, and started walking. Matt looked at Jordan, shrugged, and started following her. The rest of them fell in line, Jasper in the back.

They trudged off road most of the time now that they had abandoned the truck. It was hard going sometimes, but still, they were in farm country. They passed fields of corn, and cows wandering wild by themselves.

Late one afternoon they decided to stop at a farmhouse when a gunshot split the air, echoing around them. The bullet hit the ground at Naomi's feet. "Alright, no need to get upset," Naomi said, "We go somewhere else. It's all good."

They turned and kept walking down the road, confident another option would turn up.

That night they spent in a different farmhouse, one that was closer to a mansion. It had a very large outdoor pool, now full of dirt and leaves, and a well that couldn't draw water due to lack of power. They distilled water from the pool over a wood stove that was in the house and filled up all their water containers. Like most farmhouses, this one had a fair bit of food in stock. Still no paper maps though.

Days stretched into weeks. The group kept heading north and west. Their wounds started to heal, but they were moving slowly. Infection was a constant risk, and the whipping had left deep tissue bruises. It hurt to draw breath. Jasper had been whipped the worst, so he was the last to heal. Every breath was agony.

They were running into zombies by the ones and two, and even then not often. Sometimes they would go a few days without spotting a zombie. With so few, they were not a real threat. This was the sticks, the backwoods of the province. Most of the homes were derelict. Even before the world ended nobody lived out here.

They almost started to relax. Jasper thought it was late September and the nights were starting to get colder, but the days were beautiful for the most part and the leaves were just starting to change colour. The bugs had started to die off over the colder nights, but they still had lazy flies buzzing near them during the day. There were fields of ripe corn, golden in the sun. As they passed orchards brimming with unpicked apples they ate their fill. It was almost peaceful if you ignored the diminishing food stores, the constant exhaustion from walking all day, and the occasional zombie that wandered close enough for them to need to put it down. Jasper was feeling broken, like he had nothing left to give. He wanted to push on, to try and reach Taylor faster, but he didn't know how to make himself do it anymore.

Finally, they reached the ocean. They were almost out of supplies and exhausted. The weather began to take a turn for the worse. Rain was starting to come down hard. At first, they thought they had reached a river, the visibility was so bad. There was a bridge across part of the harbour, blocked by two sets of burnt out cars, and some bodies in between them, also burnt and blackened. The cars appeared to have been set up as a barrier, a place to trap people, or zombies, as they crossed. They couldn't see very far. It wasn't until they got on the bridge that they realized it was actually the coast, the area was covered in steep hills limiting visibility as much as the rain was.

The ocean looked leaden and angry. Dark waves occasionally whipping into white caps, and the rain was lashing down stronger. They had liberated rain gear from the farm outside of Truro but were all soaked to the skin anyway. The rain was cold, and the wind was strong. They saw a sign for Tatamagouche. Their goal, at least the short term one. Jasper had gradually drifted into the lead again, not by any sort of design, mostly by walking a bit faster, knowing the area a little bit. Naomi kept them on track, so it was usually the two of them side by side, with the rest of the group splayed out behind them.

Jasper said, "I think we need to find a place for the night, ride out the storm. Tatamagouche is small, shouldn't be too many zombies," yelling to be heard over the wind and rain.

The group agreed and they started into town on the main road, passing a burnt out car dealership and a couple of houses. One of them had burned to the ground, the other showed signs of fire, but was still mostly whole. There was a sign by the side of the road, clean and intact, as if it was still being maintained. It read "Train Station Inn Country Inn Shop Eat Sleep" and pointed to the entrance to a small side road. Jasper said, "Let's try it. Maybe it's still intact."

Jasper led them down the road just as the first crack of lightning hit. The deep rumble of the thunder filled the air, already thick with the sound of spitting rain. They could hardly see, water streaming down faces. Then they saw the Inn. It was dark, yet somehow inviting. There was a train behind it that didn't look like it had moved in many decades.

They walked up to the inn and tried the door. It was unlocked. As they opened the door they were greeted by a warm light, cheery and friendly, emanating from a pair of oil lanterns hanging from the wall. They appeared to be in gift shop/lobby area. There was a plump older woman behind the counter, grey hair tucked into an old fashioned bonnet. She had on square spectacles and an old fashioned dress, something right out of the Victorian era.

"Hello. Would you like a room for the night?"

They were taken off guard, first, no light had shone through to the outside and they had not expected a person. Second, the inside was warm and dry. There was a large wood stove, clearly retrofitted into the space, against one wall.

"Um... yes?" Jasper said.

"Alright, you look a fright. Let's get you taken care of. Don't worry, things being what they are the rooms are free. We would like a bit of help if you don't mind though. Need to make sure the place stays ship shape. Come on, upstairs with you, let's get you settled."

The woman talked in a singsong accent, somewhere in the UK Jasper figured, and she didn't seem to need to breathe from the amount she talked. Finally, she said, "Well, look at me now. All talking your poor ears off. Sorry, it's just we haven't really had any guests since the dead started walking. I miss the people you know? Normally we would be closing for the season right about now, but there's nowhere else to go really, and the walls here are good and strong. Harry and Mason make sure the zombies don't build up too much then, good lads that they are, and people need a place when the road gets too hard."

She led them up to the second floor and into a room that was completely unexpected. It was a Victorian sitting room with three doors off of it. There was a piano in the room, and all of the furniture appeared to be authentic period antiques. "Don't suppose any of you play do you? Would be so nice to have some music. Don't worry, the walls here are thick, won't carry to the outside. No? No worries. Just nice to have new faces, hear some new voices."

The three doors all led to bedrooms. The rooms had fireplaces in them, although it appeared that they had been recently modified. Each room had a double bed, and one room had a day bed as well. "Sorry about the fireplaces. They do work, but the rooms get a bit smokey. They converted them to electric a while back, so we had to tear out the electric and hook them back into the chimney. No grid means we do things the old way. Harry is good with masonry. Funny enough Mason isn't. Like I said, good lads. Supper is in an hour, we have a hog on the spit in the kitchen, so lots for all. Come down once you're settled." With that, she was off, never even having given her name.

The group stood in shock for a few minutes, then started getting settled for the night. "Watches? Who wants to keep a lookout while the rest of us get dry?" Jasper said.

Jordan volunteered, he usually did.

They discovered that each room had a washroom of sorts, although only two of the washrooms were full baths. The third was just a toilet and a sink. Each washroom had a large bucket of water. The reason was evident as soon as they turned on the taps. The place didn't have running water. The fireplaces were also empty, although each one had dry wood, some tinder, some paper, and a box of long matches.

They were suspicious and cautious, but they also needed to get warm and dry, so they started a fire in the largest of three bedrooms and stripped. By this point, none of them was shy around the others. There was a large pot in the room as well. They heated water in it and set their clothes in front of the fire. Each room had towels and a pair of soft white robes, so they dried off and put on the robes. Afterwards, Jordan took his turn. He looked a little blue. It was one of the most surreal experiences of Jasper's life. One reason for that was the windows. They were boarded up, and the boards were covered with thick black paper. They were completely light tight. The place was lit with oil lanterns and candles, helping to create a cosy atmosphere.

Jasper felt sleepy as soon as he got warm, and was fighting to stay awake. Only the thought of hot food downstairs was keeping him on his feet.

None of them had the energy to get changed back into real clothes. They all tucked small weapons into the pockets of the robes though and went downstairs to find food.

The smell was amazing as soon as the door opened, roast pork and vegetables, with a hint of spices. The old woman greeted them. "Sorry, forgot to mention. My name is Susan. I guess my husband I are the owners of the Inn now. I used to work the guest shop while Jim did odd repairs. After the zombies came our son started working with us. They lived just down the road. We have some livestock nearby, our daughter keeps the farm. Mason, our son in law is a good lad as well, handy as anything most of the time, keeps the place ship shape. Wendy will be joining us with her husband Brent."

The dining room had originally been a restaurant, but all the tables were pushed together in the centre of the room, making a single long table for them to use.

The hog was whole, head intact. It even had an apple in its mouth. There was dark bread, cheese, butter, it was a feast. The best meal Jasper could recall eating. As they ate they got to know their hosts a bit.

Occasionally someone who wasn't Susan would speak, but for the most part, it was her. Jim was a somewhat taciturn older man, physically fit and wiry. There were three younger men, Harry who looked a lot like his father Jim, Harry's husband Mason, and Brent. Mason was trim and well dressed, almost impeccable despite the end of the world, while Brent was shabby, obviously more used to working a field than sitting a table. The final member of the family was Wendy. Plump, much like her mother, with clear skin and arresting blue eyes. Her and Brent seemed completely lost in each other, madly in love. The family looked happier than anyone the group had seen since the end of the world.

"We know this is a lot to take in, always is. You folks are welcome as long as you want, but in payment for dinner and lodging, we have a few larger chores that need tending. The boys can do it, but many hands make light work and all that. Tomorrow it's going to be moving a tree off the back of the roof. I know you probably couldn't see it today, the weather being what it is, but it could get bad if we don't deal with it soon. There are a couple of other tasks. Jim has an idea for setting up a gravity flow water system, needs a big tank hoisted with muscle power. Eventually, he thinks we can get ourselves set up for hot showers again. Sorry you missed out on that, it seems like heaven on earth to me, the idea of a hot shower. Look at me, talking my fool head off again. Eat, eat."

After supper, it took moments for them to fall asleep. They meant to set a watch, but never got to it. Each room had a fire by that point, and between the food and the warmth, they were out cold almost immediately.

They woke the next day a bit later than usual. Jasper was groggy, fighting his way to consciousness. The darkness of the room was a major factor, but so was their long term exhaustion. They dressed and headed downstairs. Susan had a large pot of oatmeal bubbling on the wood stove, fresh berries and cream on the sideboard. There was also a pitcher of maple syrup and a pot of honey to use as sweeteners. "Eat. We have lots and lots. It's not like any of it will keep for long. We just had a little bit of a harvest, so this is harvest bounty. There's a couple of cows as well," Susan kept talking the entire time they ate. After breakfast, the group headed out to help move the tree.

The tree was a small one, but it was resting on the roof of the inn, putting pressure on the shingles. The family had set up a block and tackle, so the job was hard labour pulling ropes and making sure they didn't slip. Even Naomi pitched in. After the tree was moved they switched their effort and the block and tackle to a large steel tank. Jim said, "It's four hundred litres. Boys liberated it from an empty farm down the road."

There was a wooden platform and some connectors built on the roof already. They lifted the tank and nudged it in place, then a second one of the same size, and finally a two hundred litre tank went into a niche that was partially sunk into the roof. The two hundred litre tank was fed from one of the four hundred litre ones. "Bit left to do, it's all detail work though. Don't need a big crowd for that. You folks made this a lot easier," Jim said.

They had a final meal at the Inn. Susan surprised them with a change of clothes each. Not only were the clothes in good repair, they were very close to the correct size. Simple outdoor clothing, the kind used by hikers. "There's an outfitter in town. A lot of tourists used to come through here, and there's trails around. The place was empty when the change happened. I got the back door unlocked a few weeks ago and now we get all our clothes from there. It's so nice to have guests again. Are you sure you don't want to stay on?"

"Sorry, my daughter was in Charlottetown when it happened," Jasper said, "I need to get there and find out if she's okay. Have you checked the Centre yet?"

The Tatamagouche Centre was the kind of place that would be well stocked with food.

Mason said, "Yeah, I went in a while back. There was a group of hippies, doing some new age thing. Nice folks. All of them were turned. It took me a week to take care of all of them. It should be empty now, but I haven't bothered to check it out in too much detail. We aren't lacking for anything, it's just us in the town."

The journey through town was much, much less tense than expected. There were very few zombies, only the occasional roamer. Mason had a compound bow and appeared to be an exceptionally good shot. He didn't talk much, it seemed that nobody who spent time with Susan did. Maybe it was just that she was using up their entire quota of words by herself.

They moved through the town and out the other side. There was a small road with a broken down sign listing the Tatamagouche Centre on it. The sign was almost impossible to see, the grass had grown tall around it. At the end of the road was the building. It was low and long, obviously built in the seventies. The parking lot was full of dead cars, broken down and beaten by the weather.

They raided the property. It was dark inside the main building, claustrophobic. The windows should have allowed in lots of light, but they were covered in fallen branches and dirt. The stench inside hit them like a wall. Rot and death were everywhere. They saw signs that the building was being used by huge numbers of rodents. Jasper was worried that the rodents would have destroyed all the food stores, but apparently, they were too busy chewing on the corpses that littered the centre to bother with harder to access things. The kitchen contained large amounts of canned goods, all untouched.

Jasper was happy about the time they had spent in the inn despite the delay. The group was stronger, well fed. He was worried about what would happen when the weather got colder, they were in the best time for harvest, food was plentiful, and even so, they went hungry sometimes. Once snow fell they would need warmth, supplies, shelter.

He kept those thoughts to himself, trying to put on a good show, to look like he was still okay.

He was increasingly worried about Robert as well. There were only so many paths to PEI, and who knew how fast Robert might be moving? There was no question the soldiers had better weaponry. Sure, they had a couple of hunting rifles, but Robert and his group had bows if they wanted to stay silent and assault rifles if they didn't mind making noise.

One day Naomi heard horses. "Something coming. Get off the road," she said.

They got off the path and hid in the bushes, staying low to the ground. Jasper kept his eyes on the road, ready to stand up and let the riders know he was there, depending on who they were. Once he saw it was Robert he got even lower to the ground.

Robert looked awful. His face had developed scabs and sores. He was twitching and moving constantly. The rest of the soldiers and Mona looked about to collapse from the strain, but Robert didn't even look tired. Jasper huddled closer to the ground, waiting for the horse to pass by. As much as he wanted, ached, yearned, to kill Robert for what he did to Snow he owed it to the people with him and to the possibility that Taylor was still alive to keep going.

They stayed in place for about an hour after Robert passed, then Jasper said, "I don't want to chance running into them again. Their guns would make short work of us in the open, we need to make sure they don't get the chance."

Matt said, "Let's stick offroad. It's slow, but the horses can't do it, and if we stay a ways off the road we will probably spot them long before they spot us."

"I don't like the delay. It's getting colder, the longer we spend on the road the worse the weather will be. If anything is going to kill us it's going to be the weather in this fucking province."

"Yeah, fair, but the brush is pretty thin right now. Not like this is rainforest or something, and getting shot seems like an even worse plan."

"Okay, I can admit when I'm wrong. Yeah, the woods it is."

If Jasper had been willing to look directly at what he was feeling he would have realized that he had almost given up hope of reaching Taylor alive. He was going through the motions, but he didn't have much left inside. He was still moving because he felt a sense of responsibility to the small group who had followed him back at Roberts camp. Most of the forward momentum was coming from Naomi at this point. Every time he was slow to get moving in the morning she was pushing him to get moving. Every time he wanted to stop for the night hours before they needed to she pushed them on.

The season wore on, and the weather got worse. Travel was a crawl, a constant drudgery. They were far from populated areas, and food was scarce on the coast. It was rocky, and the forests were sparse, wind swept trees. They found berries occasionally, not much else. The only positive was that the lack of population meant they didn't run into many zombies.

One day they were pushing through high cliffs. There was a road that ran between the cliffs and the ocean, winding past crashing surf. The sun was high in the sky, sea birds calling out to each other. They were tired and hadn't seen anyone for weeks. Food was again low, this time desperately so, and they were incredibly hungry. They had rationed themselves with far, far less food than they needed. That was probably why they took the blind curve without really paying attention. On the other side of the curve was a cluster of more than twenty zombies. They were wandering aimlessly. All of them were dressed in suits or dresses, church clothing. The cluster started moving toward them, shuffling as fast as they were able.

The group backed up, then turned and started running. The zombies kept following though, too close to lose easily.

The road was in very poor repair. It probably hadn't seen maintenance in a decade or two, and it was pitted all over the place. Jordan hit a pothole badly and went sprawling on the ground. Jasper turned, trying to get back to him, but the zombies were on him before Jasper could reach him. One of the creatures bit deep into Jordan's calf, blood spurting everywhere. Jasper turned back around and started running again.

Jordan's death gave the group some space, an extra moments lead time, as the zombies stopped to eat him. The group was stuck on a narrow road, with zombies behind them and dozens of kilometres before the cliffs ended.

Matt spotted a break in the cliff face. Not exactly clear, but climbable. He started up, climbing quickly. "This way, hurry!"

The others followed. Jasper was the last one to start up the cliff, only a few feet up when the zombies came around the bend. Jasper sped up, climbing faster and faster. His hand slipped, as a shower of rock fell down on his head. He slipped down the cliff side, sliding towards the road below, and the waiting zombies. He managed to get his left hand around something solid and felt a strong pull on his shoulder as his arm held him in place. He kept a hold somehow, shoulder straining, almost separating, and found himself hanging by one arm, feet inches above the outstretched arms below him. The smell of the zombies wafted up to him, a mix of stale shit, urine, and fresh blood.

Jasper tried to find some purchase for his feet, and for his other hand. He didn't have enough strength to hold for long. Even if he got both hands on it, it would only be a matter of minutes before his grip failed. He needed a foot hold. His feet were flailing through empty space, panic was setting in. Finally, he got his foot against something solid and he was able to take some of the strain off of his arm. It gave him enough time that he was able to calm down, to find another hand hold, another foothold. He started back up the cliff.

At the top Sasha was crying. "Oh God. Jordan," she said with a sob.

They allowed themselves a few minutes to grieve, then took stock of their situation. They were on top of a cliff, with no cover. Jordan had been carrying the travel pack when he went down, so they no longer had their tarps or sleeping bags, and the majority of their rations. The landscape they were on was rock. They could see some scrub brush far in the distance, but there was almost no shelter. It was late in the day, with night coming earlier these days. There was a strong chill in the air.

"Okay, so we're fucked," Jasper said, "We have nothing, and I don't have a clue how to deal with this landscape."

Naomi started picking up what little equipment they had left. "We'll get it. This shit ain't it. We ain't going out like this. Just get your lazy asses up and fucking walk. You think Jordan wants us dyin' here?"

They started walking along the cliff, heading for where the scrub brush started. They probably wouldn't survive the night if they didn't get some form of shelter. Food and water would have to wait.

There was a large rock jutting out of the landscape, with a small hollow at its base. The hollow was about six feet across and partially covered. It looked like their best bet. It was dry at the bottom, a small channel open to take any rain out so they wouldn't drown in their sleep.

They shoved their bodies in as tightly as they could manage, relying on each other for warmth and shelter.

The night passed and they didn't die. The temperature stayed above freezing, and they were wearing layers. Without mutual body heat, they would not have made it to morning.

The next day they didn't talk, just walked. Eventually, they found a point where the rocks gave way to gentler terrain. There was a stream, just a small one running out of the rocks. They drank from it, not caring if it was safe by that point.

They were drained, the water gave them a tiny bit of life, but not enough. They were starving to death, and with so much of their gear gone, their numbers reduced, they were closer to the edge. Something in Jasper came together at that moment. His resolve, ever weakening since the day Snow was killed, came back. This wasn't it for him. Whether Taylor was alive or not, he wasn't going to die.

They were starving. Sleep was a challenge, and water was scarce. Shelter was rare. They travelled all day every day, never pausing. They slept where they could, any tiny nook or cranny. Hollow logs, ditches, anything that provided even a wind break. Shelter was their most immediate priority, water a close second, but in the background was the knowledge that they were taking in less than two hundred calories a day. There was no way they could survive on that. Their gums were starting to bleed, and they all had joint pain. If they didn't get some food soon they were dead. They were too weak to fight almost any threat, and near the end of their ability to forage. The weather had turned cold, every morning the ground had a layer of white over it, the dirt hard and crisp. It was too wet for easy fire, and Jasper's hands were so cold they shook whenever he tried to carve out heartwood, he couldn't get anything to take a spark. The early days of the journey where the weather was a friend and days brought warmth were a distant memory. Nobody was even sure what month it was. Probably into November given the weather, but maybe late October. Jasper was sure that Taylor was dead, that his quest had been hopelessly naive. Didn't matter though, he would grieve later, he owed Naomi, Matt, Candice, and Sasha.

One day dawned grey, almost like it never dawned at all. The sky was cloudy and angry, rain drizzling down. It was a cold rain, the kind that saps strength and hope, leaving you feeling chilled to the bone. Naomi was shivering so badly she could barely put one foot in front of the other. She was stumbling, dizzy. Jasper noticed after a while when she sat down on a rock and started to take off her jacket. He stopped her and pulled her to her feet. He had enough training to know that she was in fairly severe hypothermia. She had always been the smallest of the group, and now she was severely undernourished as well. She didn't have enough reserves on her small frame. If they didn't find shelter, warmth, and food soon she wasn't going to make it.

"Guys, I have to do a scout. Naomi is pretty much done, freezing to death. Huddle close to her, huddle together. I have to find someplace to keep us warm, don't let her freeze to death while I do it, okay? Good."

Over the next few hours, he scouted far and wide, looking for something they could use. The woods were thick, but most of the leaves were gone. He spotted a trail eventually, it looked like it had been maintained until the zombies hit. There were still trail markers in the trees, bits of brightly coloured plastic, signs of the old world. Following the trail seemed like the best option, these places usually led somewhere, and that was better than what he had to work with. Near dusk he saw a building through the trees, a log shape, blending into the forest. It was better than he could have expected, a ranger way station, the doors left unlocked for any traveller who came upon it. The way station had a few minimal supplies, a veritable feast to the group. It also had a wood stove with dry wood, some blankets, comfy if minimal furniture. The trip back to the group was a nightmare, it was hard to see the marking he had made on the trees as he left, and it started to rain harder, a cold bone chilling rain mixed with sleet. By the time he reached them Naomi was unconscious.

"I found a cabin, it has food. Help me get Naomi up, let's go."

Matt grabbed Naomi's legs, swaying badly himself. He was in almost as bad shape as she was. Jasper lifted her under the shoulders, gasping with effort. How could someone so small feel so heavy?

They trudged through the woods, managing to keep their way. Naomi's breathing was shallow, her dark skin gone pale. Jasper kept hold of her shoulders the whole way. When Matt stumbled and dropped her Sasha took her legs, while Candice held Matt up.

Jasper made a fire as soon as he got in. The place warmed up rapidly, chasing the cold out of their bodies. After a few minutes, Naomi started to stir. There was an old tin of carnation hot chocolate on the shelf, about half full. There were a pair of tin mugs and plates in addition to an old pot. They took turns with the mugs, Jasper gave Naomi and Matt the first round.

Jasper put together a simple meal, something to get some calories in them. They settled on Kraft Dinner with canned spam. In the old world Jasper wouldn't have touched that with a ten-foot pole, but at this point, it might as well have been a seven-course meal at a five-star restaurant.

Slowly their strength came back. They were woefully under dressed for the weather, of course. They had been on the road for too long, since summer, on foot almost the whole time. Properly equipped the walk should have taken two months or so, but they weren't any of those things. It was getting so cold out, beyond what they could manage with what they had. This was a way station, so there wasn't much there beyond the food and furniture. A couple of ratty old blankets that weren't useful for travel, but at least they provided some cover while they were there.

One thing that was there was a paper map. Even better, whoever had left the map had left a mark on the cabin, so they even knew exactly where they were. They were in Amherst Shore Provincial Park, a small park with some camping. The New Brunswick border was only a day or two away, and the bridge just a week or two past that. Hell, the bridge itself was as long as the trip from where they were to the New Brunswick border.

They stayed put until the food was gone. They talked about carrying supplies with them, but in the end, they needed the rest enough that it was worth the wait. Fire and hot food for a few days made a massive difference.

They headed out of the shelter. Now that they knew which direction to take they quickly found themselves outside of the forest, looking at some small roads and some houses. Not many, just a few. This wasn't a heavily populated area.

The map showed a few small communities nearby. They explored a bit, to see if they could find any better cold weather clothing, maybe some kind of portable shelter.

Soon they found a couple of farms. It was pretty consistent. Remote farms were the best bet for scavenging. Farmers would have stores of food most of the time, and sometimes they might have things ready for harvest, although that was getting rarer now, as the weather started to turn, most fields were full of vegetables rotting on the ground. The first farmhouse was modest, with multiple greenhouses behind it. There were large fields further back, all the crops rotted on the ground.

The group moved up to the house and tried the door. As was common in these parts the door wasn't locked. There was nobody on the ground floor, but they heard the familiar sounds of zombies locked in rooms upstairs. They decided to scavenge what they could and ignore the zombies for now. They had been there for months most likely and would stay put for at least long enough for the group to get what they needed and get out.

As usual, they were able to scrounge a decent amount of stored food. In this farm, the food tended towards homemade preserves. It was clear from the decor that the inhabitants preferred a hippie aesthetic. The place smelled strongly of patchouli. There was a lot of spoiled food in the fridge of course, and the bread was green with mould.

They searched the place and found a few backpacks, obviously hippie gear. Also some cold weather clothing in an upstairs closet. It was a weird mishmash, and oddly there were three full sets that fit Naomi and nobody else. Even Candice was a bit too big for those outfits.

For the first time, Naomi was wearing clothing that fit her, matched her body type, and looked good. In fact, she looked great, like a trust fund kid gone slumming. Matt, on the other hand, was in a jacket that was two sizes too large at least.

They raided the next three farms. Nothing was as good as the hippie house, and they had to dispatch the owners of the next two places. Feeling more alive and capable than they had in a very long time they headed out.

By sticking to the road they were able to make it across to New Brunswick in a day and a half. There was a sign letting them know they had crossed the provincial border. It felt like a letdown. They had travelled so far, endured so much, and there was just a sign by the side of the road, no stations, no border, nothing. Of course, the bridge to PEI was still a ways ahead, a week or two at least, and PEI was the real destination, but this was a milestone. They had left the Nova Scotia peninsula.

Cowboys

Robert was moving fast. The horses made them so much more efficient. It wasn't purely the speed boost, they also carried the gear, meaning the soldiers were much, much less tired.

They covered miles, occasionally running into a zombie, and once a living human. An old man who lived in a tar shack in the woods. They ignored him and he ignored them. He was so remote that they weren't even sure he knew the zombie apocalypse had happened.

As the weeks passed the landscape turned. The green started to fade to brown and orange, the grass died, became straw. The weather was still nice, until it wasn't. They got caught outside in a major storm, they couldn't get the big tents set up because of the high wind. Every time they tried the tent fabric was pulled out of their hands. In the end, they had to huddle together, horses around them, in the minimal cover provided by some trees.

The next morning the men were demoralized. Robert was frozen through, although the day did warm up quickly. Their clothes were soaked, and a couple of the men had developed coughs. A lesson in when they should stop.

Mona was quiet these days. She seemed tired. Robert was okay with that, he wasn't looking for conversation from her. She didn't have a whole lot to say at the best of times, and these weren't the best of times. So long as she was willing to go along with what he was doing he didn't really give a shit.

One of the soldiers, a guy named Steve, fell into a coughing fit two days after the storm and ended up collapsing off his horse. Robert stopped the group. As much as he needed to catch up to Jasper and the other traitors he couldn't have his men dying on horseback. They set up camp and started trying to treat the sick men. In another couple of days, it was half of them. The first one died that night. They put a spike through his skull. After that, they tied the sick up. Their numbers were too low, and he didn't have medicine for them. Nothing to do but keep them dry and warm and hope.

In the end, they lost three. Robert wasn't sure what it was, maybe pneumonia, hell, maybe TB for all he knew. Tom was one of the three, so their medical capability was minimal. Robert wondered why he didn't care, but that was something he'd become used to, so he didn't give it a whole lot of thought. Ironically Steve, the first one to fall, also managed to recover and was riding with them. He was weak though and needed frequent breaks. It felt like they were losing all the time they had managed to gain with the horses.

They hit the ocean a few days later. The north shore of the mainland. It was desolate. They started heading west, hugging the coast.

One of the horses died. Robert had been riding hard for days and one night when he stopped one of the horses just lay down, dead. Robert looked at the horses and realized that he could see their ribs, all of them. The men were ragged and thin, Mona looked like one of the corpses. All of them had dark circles under their eyes and hollowed out cheeks. It was a combination of exhaustion, dehydration, and starvation. His drive told him to keep going, but the pragmatic side of him said that they would need to find food, maybe rest for a few days. He thought they were somewhere around the New Brunswick border. There was a small wooden house, dilapidated even before things fell apart. Now it was barely more than a shell. The door was slightly ajar. Robert walked in, baton in hand. There was a zombie, an old man, probably a hermit from the look of the place. He smashed it in the head with his baton over and over again. Finally, its skull collapsed. "All clear," Robert called out to the men. They came inside. Mona followed, timid and meek.

The place was a mess. There was a stench to any space that had held a zombie for any length of time, but this place was worse than that. It was obvious that the former owner was a hoarder. Robert started tidying as soon as he got the men inside. It wouldn't do. That kind of disorder would negatively affect discipline. If they were going to stay there for a few days they would need to get it straightened up.

He worked for seven hours straight, his energy never flagging. There was a large store of canned food, mostly home preserves. The place was in rough shape, and there were some bizarre finds among the piles of detritus, including at least one dead cat. It appeared to have been dead for a long time, years probably.

He got the place sorted though, even uncovered a real bed for him and Mona to share. The men made do with the sagging sofa or a patch of floor. It was better than they had had for a very long time. Real walls, windows that closed. The door was swollen, so it didn't quite shut, but they pushed and then pushed more, and in the end it almost closed. They used chord to make sure it was held shut.

There was a large patch of grass for the horses and not another house in sight, they hadn't passed one in days either.

Robert wasn't certain exactly where they were. Somewhere in the backwoods between Nova Scotia and New Brunswick. He had a map, but it was hard to reconcile the landscape he encountered with the one on the map. Not that he wasn't experienced at navigation, but having to avoid population at every turn meant that they missed a lot of landmarks. He had learned, through bitter experience, that the main roads were usually not worth it. They had tried sticking to the highway for a while but kept having to lose zombie clusters. These back roads sometimes had signs, other times not so much. All of them were in terrible condition.

Robert settled in to rest and recover. The men were grateful for the respite, and it was clear this place hadn't had electricity before the apocalypse, so not much had changed for it. There was a tub, a well that used a bucket to haul water, a wood stove, and an outhouse. On the second day, Robert cleaned the tub and then boiled water so he could have a hot bath. It was a luxury beyond belief. He invited Mona to join him.

The men and the horses started to look better after three days. He gave them two more. The horses were more the impetus than the men. After that, they had exhausted all the food in the house, probably a winters worth for the original owner. They got on the move again, heading north.

Robert hit the bridge to PEI late in the day. It was a cold day, with clear blue skies. The few clouds were light, high wisps. The air smelled crisp and clear, the way only a fall day can. The bridge was barricaded with a bunch of vehicles, far too many to clear. Somebody had tried to fortify it, successfully from the look of things. It was going to require them to climb to get across, not something the horses were going to be able to do. Robert set up camp under the bridge putting off the decision as to what to do with the horses as long as possible.

There was a nature trail with a little visitors centre right next to them. Nothing much, just a small building with a gift shop and some displays. It had several vending machines that were untouched. Robert decided that the vending machines were free now, so he smashed in their front panels.

Most of the stuff was stale, but the pop was cold at least. Nothing worse than warm pop.

Robert set a watch on the approach to the bridge. Jasper had to come this way. Robert still wanted to punish him. The men had been disrespectful ever since Jasper left, clearly, they didn't respect his authority fully with Jasper still running around defiant. It was worth waiting a little bit before making the crossing. He also sent a man to scout the bridge itself. It was a full days journey across, and the same coming back.

They hunkered in to wait for something else to happen.

The scout on the bridge finally came back. "The bridge is clear past the barricade, no zombies, no people. Somebody set it up pretty good though."

"How so? What can we use?"

"There's a kind of fort in the middle. Two rows of cars, more stacked on top, a bus with a wood stove in the middle of them. Looks like it's meant for a garrison, but nobody there now. Far end's blocked too."

Robert decided that the bridge was an even better ambush point. It would give Jasper nowhere to run. He killed the horses, slitting their throats, wouldn't do to let anyone else get them, and he started across. The climb over the initial barrier was impossible for a zombie, but fairly easy for a human.

The journey to the centre took longer than anticipated. It started raining after they had been on the bridge for an hour, and it kept raining most of the time they were travelling. The winds picked up as well, and there was no place to get out of it. By the time they reached the barricade it was full night and all of them were freezing. Mona collapsed just shy of their destination and Robert carried her the last little bit.

They set up for the wait. The men built a small fire in the wood stove that was in the bus. The windows were covered in blankets, and some enterprising soul had actually set up a mass heater. The thing wasn't the warmest in the world, but so long as your butt was on the bench it was reasonably comfortable, and it was dry. Mona came to after a bit and Robert made sure she had some warm tea, one of the only things they had to drink other than water.

Approaching Storm

The weather was bad. Jasper and his group were moving slowly because of it. Every kilometre was a struggle. It had turned cold a few days ago, and then colder still. The pelting rain meant that all of them were soaked to the bone, bundles of sodden misery. The bridge was close though. They had spotted it from a high point a few hours back, before the rain got really, really bad. Now the visibility was terrible, limiting their world to a small sphere, the bridge far outside of it.

Jasper was shivering, a deep bone chill setting in. It was sapping his strength, almost sapping his will to live. Days like that are awful when you have a place to go, shelter, warmth. When you have no respite, no hope of respite, it's so much worse. They were discovering the lessons every frontier person, every homeless person has always known about how hard it can be when you are exhausted and chilled to your bones, you are hungry, tired, always so tired, dirty, at the edge of your resources. Jasper wanted to lie down. Wanted maybe wasn't the right term. He looked at level patches of ground with longing, like a long lost lover, like the source of all hope and light and truth in the world.

The finally hit the point where the bridge was visible again. Very close, agonizingly close. There were a few zombies clustered around the entrance, but the entrance itself was blocked. For the thousandth time, Jasper wished he had his sword back, or even better, Snow padding along silently next to him.

"Hold up. We need to wait until the rain lifts, or morning, something. I can't take any zombies right now."

"You got it boss man," Matt said, "Morning it is."

They found a sheltered spot on the approach to the bridge where they could hole up for the night. It wasn't much, a small overhang. The rain wasn't falling directly on them at least. They huddled together for warmth. They didn't want to set up any kind of shelter because it would attract zombies, and they didn't have nearly the energy to fight them.

They spent a miserable night huddled together. They were sheltered enough that they were getting warmer instead of colder, but barely. The next morning dawned still grey and empty. The zombies at the bridge had wandered off in the night, losing interest in whatever had kept them there.

They got themselves ready. Setting a fire was challenging with the wet conditions, but Jasper had carved out some heartwood and some tinder on his way, and he had taken a lighter and some cotton balls and Vaseline from one of the farmhouses. The fire breathed new life into them. Sleep had been scarce for days. At least it looked like the barricade was keeping the bridge zombie free.

They climbed over. Some of the scattered zombies headed back in their direction, but they were over long before the zombies could reach them.

The bridge was long. It had high concrete walls along the entire length, meaning that most of the time you couldn't really see the ocean if you were walking, although you could glimpse it a fair ways distant. The bridge also curved, fairly gently. It was clear of obstructions at first. After the barrier at the beginning, there were no vehicles to contend with. They walked in silence.

After a few hours of walking, Jasper spotted a second barricade. A monstrous tower of vehicles in the middle of the bridge, three cars tall. A gunshot rang out, Matt dropped like a sack, blood spurting from his thigh. There was no cover at all, just the flat deck of the bridge. Jasper ran forward, zigzagging as best he could. The rest of the group followed.

Shots kept ringing out, and Sasha fell. Then they hit the barricade. Jasper could see the rifle through a car window. He reached in and grabbed it, his heavy gloves sparing his hands from burning on the hot barrel. He pulled forward and the gun came out in his hands. There was yelling from the other side, and a second gun barrel came down over the top of the barricade. Candice,small and lithe, surged up and grabbed that gun as well. The gun came down with her, and the owner came down too. He hadn't been braced properly. Jasper recognized Steve from the camp. Candice drew a hunting knife across his throat, blood spurting along the line of the blade.

Fuck.

It was Robert obviously, and whatever remained of his forces. Of course, it was. As soon as Jasper stopped to think about it it was obvious. They were headed to the same place, they were mounted, they made it sooner. Hell, he'd seen them pass. If only he hadn't been so exhausted and overcome with hope at seeing the bridge he would have expected it, would have taken precautions. He should have been prepared, should have had weapons at the ready. He knew better, knew not to let his guard down. Now Sasha and Matt were wounded, maybe dying, maybe dead.

He looked back, saw Matt crawling forward. Sasha wasn't getting up. Naomi was at the barricade, down against the ground, using the barricade itself for what little cover it could provide.

It occurred to Jasper that if this barricade was designed against zombies some of the doors might be unlocked. He found a car in the bottom row and tried the door. It didn't open, so he tried another. The third one came open in his hands. The frame was bent and warped from the weight of the cars above it, but it opened! Jasper ducked in, holding the stolen rifle in his arm. Candice appeared to be doing the same thing, but through an open window in the second row of cars. He peered through the far window. The other side of the barricade had a bus, and five people. Mona was one of them, and Robert was another, deteriorated even further since the last time Jasper had seen him. The last three were guys he didn't know very well, other than from when they had grabbed him at the camp. All three of them looked exhausted, although Mona looked worse than any of them. Her face was badly bruised and she was back to the weight she had been when he first met her, if not even thinner.

He took aim at Robert, careful not to let the barrel stick out past the window. The angle was terrible. The roof of the car being as crushed as it was meant that he couldn't really sit up, he had to half crouch to bring the rifle barrel around, and Robert was well off to the far side of the barrier. Finally, he had the shot lined up. He took it. Robert moved just as his finger squeezed the trigger, and the shot missed - by slightly less than it would have if Robert hadn't moved. Jasper was inexperienced with guns and the shot was badly off target.

After that, things really went to hell. Robert moved in while his men opened fire. Jasper ducked down into the passenger side, as close to the floor as he could get. Bullets ripped through the side of the car, the roof, everywhere. He felt a stinging burn in his left shoulder. Finally, the bullets stopped. Jasper slowly moved up, peering through a large hole in the door. His adrenaline was coursing, making everything seem clearer, sharper. The pain in his shoulder was distant, almost a non-concern. Robert was standing, rifle aimed in his direction, clearly waiting for movement. He decided to wait it out, make them come to him. After a few minutes with nothing happening, Robert said, "Go check it out. I think we got the motherfucker. Let's see you come back from that one asshole!"

One of the men went to check on Jasper's car. The man made his way up the barricade.

Jasper drew his knife and waited. Hunched over the blade so his bloody shoulder showed, and the knife was hidden. He hoped he would look like a corpse until the man was too close to do anything.

The door opened. "Hey, we got the fucker. He's dead".

"Make sure," Robert said.

The soldier started poking Jasper with the barrel of his gun. Jasper stayed limp even though the hot metal burned him. The soldier moved the barrel aside and reached out with his left hand to check Jasper's pulse. Jasper spun up and slammed the blade of his knife into the man's windpipe while grabbing his rifle. He gurgled and foamy blood started to trickle down his throat. Jasper backed out of the car, taking the extra rifle with him. He was worried about Candice. He hadn't seen or heard anything from her since she made her way into the car. Nothing he could do though.

The barricade was a great defence against zombies, but poorly designed for human opponents. It didn't exactly give Jasper and his group an advantage, but not a major disadvantage either. All the car bodies that became murder holes when dealing with the undead were just cover with openings on both sides when dealing with humans carrying guns.

Jasper made his way along the surface to the same corner Matt had crawled to. Naomi had made it over to Matt as well. Sasha was still down, not moving.

They heard movement from the other side of the barricade. Matt was breathing ragged and shallow, lending even more urgency to Jasper's mind. Jasper realized that he only had one play left. He needed another car with an open door and a gas tank on his side of the barrier. He found one after a few minutes. The door didn't open, but the window didn't exist and it was enough. He climbed in, silently and popped the gas tank. No idea how much gas was in the vehicle, but if there was anything it should work.

He moved slowly, painfully slowly, to get out. He could hear climbing on the other side of the barricade, he knew he needed to be faster than them. He got out and called to Candice, "Get the fuck out of there. NOW!".

She did as he asked, dropping to the bridge deck quickly. Jasper took out a lighter and piece of cotton ball he had coated with Vaseline. He lit it and dropped it into the gas tank. It sounded like whoever was climbing was almost to the top.

For a minute it seemed like nothing was going to happen, then he heard a whoomph and flames shot out of the tank. A second later they shot out of the hood, catching the fill material. The smell was horrible, an overwhelming odour of chemicals burning. The acrid smoke spread fast. Jasper grabbed Matt and started pulling him away. The flames spread fast. In minutes half the cars were on fire.

There were a few small explosions, not big Hollywood ones, just little ones as gas heated and the pressure blew the tanks. A few cars fell on each side, still burning. The flames kept growing hotter and hotter, they had to back off. Once they reached Sasha Candice checked her pulse. Nothing. She was dead already. They left her there and backed off even further. Matt was shot in the leg, but he was bleeding heavily and showing symptoms of shock. Jasper did his best, put pressure on the wound, tried to wake him up enough to get some sugar into him. In a few minutes Matt's breathing took on a different tone, then it stopped.

There was no way they could get to the barricade. The flames were hundreds of feet high. There was also probably no way back. All the light would attract zombies, and while they probably couldn't get through the barricade at the shore side of the bridge anytime soon, they would be clustered around it, in huge numbers. Eventually, the barricade would fall by sheer weight of numbers, and they would need to be gone by then.

The fire burned for hours. Jasper stayed close enough to be warmed by it. Luckily the wind was carrying the smoke away from them, over to Robert's side of the bridge. That also meant that providing it burnt out before the zombies got to his group he should be able to make it across, Robert would have to back off if he survived the smoke and the firestorm. They waited because there was nothing else they could do.

Darkness fell, but the barricade still burned. Lower now, but hot. So very hot. At some point in the night, they heard a cracking sound, and part of the deck under the barricade failed. Chunks of concrete fell, surrounded by glowing steel. This bridge, another marvel of the modern age, spanning twelve kilometres of open ocean, was failing just months after humanity did.

Cars fell as the pile shifted, sliding off the ends into the ocean. The barricade was thinner, more tenuous now.

When the fire finally went out it got cold. The rain was still falling, unrelenting. Jasper had been ignoring the wound in his shoulder so far, but it was hurting, burning, on fire with pain. "Naomi. I need you to check my shoulder. I don't know how bad it is."

The bullet had passed through muscle, but it was bleeding. Naomi bandaged it as best she could with what they had.

They approached the former barricade. The surface asphalt was burned off in many places, and the concrete was so badly warped from the heat that you could see through to the ocean in many places. As they approached the vehicles they felt the heat still radiating from them. The ground was hot. They used that, found a point where it was warming them up, and waited for the heat to dissipate. That way they slowly made it to the barricade. At one point a piece of decking fell as they stepped near it, so they slowed down even more. They could see the rebar in many of the gaps, set close together. They followed the path of the rebar, using it to help ensure they wouldn't fall through if some of the deck failed. Finally, they climbed over the burnt out shells of the vehicles.

On the other side, the bus had burnt as well. It was no more than a shell of a vehicle. Probably too close to the barricade, which wasn't much of a barricade anymore, although still a good zombie deterrent with the missing pieces of deck and what amounted to pit traps leading straight into the ocean. The burnt out shell of a bus didn't offer much in the way of warmth, and they were rapidly freezing to death. It was a few degrees above zero, and the rain was mixed with sleet. The cold was once again their biggest enemy.

Aftermath

Robert fled the fire, Mona and his last remaining soldier in tow. There was no way this was going to pass. He was going to find a way to kill Jasper, no matter what. It wouldn't be now though, there would be a better opportunity. For now, he needed to stay alive, to stay mobile. If your ambush point fails, move to another one, never let your opponent choose the battleground. Jasper had changed the tenor of the conflict with that fire. The far end of the bridge might work... at least he thought so until he got there.

It was full of zombies. They were laid out three deep. All told he thought there were a couple hundred of them. No way to go back, no supplies left to speak of, nothing to do but try to thin the mass of zombies. He drew his sword, it used to be Jasper's, way better than a machete for the purpose and climbed on top of the barricade. He started to swing down at the zombie's heads.

After an hour his arms failed. He couldn't swing anymore, so he went to the other side of the barricade and took a break. He repeated this process until there were no zombies on the other side. They were unable to reach him where he was, and he had the reach to hit them. The thing about zombies is they don't change tactics when the old ones aren't working.

After that, they made their way over the barricade and found a place to collapse. The small town was empty, no people, no wandering zombies. Robert picked a building with an open door since that meant the zombies were probably lying dead next to the barricade.

They rested for the night. Robert half wanted to wait, but there were no supplies here. The place had been ransacked, and his group had almost no water. They needed to find fresh water quickly. All three of them had been throwing up as a result of the toxic smoke the day before. No way of knowing how long Jasper would wait. Robert gave the little anarchistic fuck credit for brains. He was a good tactician, even if he had no sense of discipline.

There was only one more point where he had a good chance of ambushing Jasper, right outside of Charlottetown. It wasn't the only way into town, but it was the most likely one.

They started out into the countryside, looking for farmhouses with obvious wells.

Into the Tame

Jasper, Naomi, and Candice hit the barrier on the island side as the first snow began to fall. It was just a few light flurries, but it was cold. The sheer number of bodies dead by the barrier was staggering. It was hundreds, too many to make sense of. All with their heads destroyed.

They walked into the town, looking for anywhere they could use for warmth. They looked through windows. Many of the houses still housed undead occupants, but they were looking for someplace with an obvious fireplace or wood stove. The couple of zombies inside wouldn't be a major concern.

The entire province had a quarter the population of Halifax, and most of the space was taken up by farms. There weren't very many people.

They found a place with a large wood pile stacked in the driveway. "Here," Jasper said, trying the knob. It was unlocked. They opened the door cautiously. Nothing came at them. There was an old wood stove in the living room. The place was cold of course, it had been empty for many months, and the condition showed it. The kitchen window was smashed in. The back door was open, although the screen door was closed. The screen door pushed out. Jasper figured the inhabitants probably walked out it and then when it closed behind them couldn't get back in. Good for him and his group. They could see a fenced yard a few houses away with a pair of zombies trying to get out.

Nobody felt like talking. They were too shaken, the grief too present, too recent.

They closed the main door and stoked a fire. After the place started to warm up they did a search, room by room. It was empty. Just a small home, portraits of a number of children, probably enough that they were grandkids. Also photos of an older couple. There were commemorative plates, commemorative spoons, commemorative mugs, hundred and hundreds of salt and pepper shakers. The furniture was mostly overstuffed and old, and the whole place still, despite being open to the elements, had a lingering smell of stale cigarettes. There were stand ashtrays next to every piece of furniture. Still, the place was warming up quickly.

They found some plywood in the basement and placed it over the window, cutting out the wind and the snow. There were some tins of food down there, and a case of bottled water. It was the cheap kind, lots and lots of small bottles, but better than nothing.

They set up a meal around the stove, cooking tinned soup with bottled water. There were saltines to break up in the soup. It tasted like heaven, like the greatest meal ever made. Jasper wanted to plan, to figure out what they were going to do, but he didn't have the energy or the knowledge. There was also a tin of hot chocolate mix. Something that they had found in most of the homes they had raided. They made hot chocolate with more of the bottled water, then fell asleep on the living room floor in the warmth of the wood stove.

The next morning they got serious about raiding the community. It was pretty badly stripped. The house they were in was one of the few with any food in it, and then it was just the little bit in the basement, a single medium sized box.

They did manage to get some water though. Mostly just collected rainfall. There were empty containers, nobody bothered to take those. "A car would speed the hell out of this bitch," Naomi said, "We could make Charlottetown before that motherfucker." Nobody had to ask who she meant.

They tried every car they could find. Most didn't have keys, and of the few that did none would start. It had been months that the vehicles had sat idle. Batteries only last so long, and gasoline goes bad.

They did manage to find a few small things. One SUV had a cache of protein bars in the trunk, one house had a couple of shotguns - small twenty gauge ones, not exactly high on stopping power. Some more bottled water tucked in the back of a convenience store. Everything else edible was gone.

It was clear this area wasn't going to be much use to them, so they started on the road to Charlottetown. Naomi was navigating again. They also used the highway as a signpost, giving them a general route. Traveling in PEI was a tradeoff. The weather was awful, and the wind was extreme, nothing to break the wind as it sped off the ocean. It was costing them time because the cold was so severe... but it was also easier terrain. Everything was flat, and there was no forest to speak of. They were able to see a great distance most of the time and were able to spot zombies long before they came close - except when the wind, rain, and occasional snow, got so bad they could barely see at all.

They travelled for days, and then weeks. In all that time they saw nobody living, until one day they were searching for shelter, it was just hitting twilight, leaving it really close to their limit, and they spotted lights. Real, actual, electric lights. They hurried forward, wind whipping them, punishing them for every step. All of them had managed to find clothing, but it was mostly just layers upon layers. They had passed the point of noticing their stink. Electric light meant humans, meant civilization.

There was a small building, and behind it a fenced in area. The fenced in area was several hundred metres. It contained ramshackle huts, hastily constructed. The fence also had zombies around it. Lots of them. The zombies were tied to heavy stakes sticking out of the ground, straining against their ropes but too stupid to slip them. The ropes were tied around their waist and neck. The main building appeared to be a restaurant/convenience store. There were zombies on the approach to it as well, but there was a clear channel running through them. Obviously meant to channel people into a small area.

It was late enough that Jasper decided to chance it. Despite the experience with Robert he still believed that most people would be trying to stick together, to make the species survive. Plus he was willing to trade protein bars for shelter if need be.

As they approached the door a young woman stuck her head out of a second story window. She had a rifle in her hands, just a bolt action twenty-two, but not something Jasper wanted pointed his way. "Stop. Lay down any weapons you have. We don't want to hurt you, but we have to make sure you can't hurt us."

They did as the woman commanded, laying down gear and guns. Jasper even took out the spare knife he had in his boot. A couple of men came out and frisked them. The men looked rough. Lean and dangerous, long beards over dirty faces. They searched the group and then beckoned them to follow.

Inside the place was lit. They could hear a humming sound that was clearly a generator. It was a restaurant, and there were people at the tables. They were eating, drinking coffee, talking. There were even a few waitresses, dressed in blue dresses with aprons, running around taking orders and topping up cups. The entire scene was surreal, like running into a live Dali painting. The men beckoned Jasper and his crew to the convenience store side. Inside it was very different. The place had been emptied of shelving, and there was a large table with chairs around it. An older man and woman were there. Both were large and looked extremely strong. Hard working farm types. "I'm Beth. This is my place. This is Conrad".

"I'm Jasper, these two are Naomi and Candice. Pleased to meet you."

"You folks look pretty rough," Beth asked, "You had a hard time of it I take it?"

Jasper told her about his journey, from start to finish. He didn't want to leave out any details, there were potential consequences for Beth and her people from things he had done, and he wanted to make sure they were prepared. There were too few people left to let his pride endanger any of them.

"Well shit, we had some issues, but I guess we had it pretty easy compared to you folks. I used to live right near here, Conrad was in the area too. I mean we lost people, of course, but I think I had to travel all of ten klicks. I came here to raid the place, couple days after the zombies showed up. Found out it had a working genny, lots of spare gas. Hell, the freezer was still working, full of food. Set up shop right away. Conrad came by couple days later. He built most of the compound out back. We were friends before, so I trusted him right off."

"Wow, sounds like you guys hit a bit of luck."

"Damn right. Once I found the owner I knew the place was mine. He was up in the apartment above the restaurant, trying his darndest to eat my brains. Never did like the old lech. Used to hit on the waitresses something fierce. Anyway, as we were setting up a couple boys came up and tried to take over. Conrad took a bullet, but he bashed both their brains in with a hammer. After I got him patched up we started collecting the zombies, made a good deterrent to folks who wanted to sneak up on us. We're still open to newcomers though. We got plenty of food, this area's all farms, enough food that we got ourselves set for the winter and had to leave most of it on the ground. Tried our best to save the livestock too, but had to butcher more of it than we wanted. We let the ones we couldn't use or care for go. Careful, lots of wild cows roaming around this winter..."

"You seem to have picked up a few extras."

"Yeah, lots of em' I figure everyone with a pulse in a hundred klicks stopped in here at some point. Not your Robert fellow though, I'm glad of that. We like newcomers, folks who can do different things. Anyone who stays more n' a day or two we expect to pitch in, build themselves a place, help keep up the community. New faces though, it's enough that you bring news with you, or even just stories we ain't heard bout a hundred times already."

"Do you have any idea what Charlottetown is like?"

"Yeah, had a few come through from there a few days ago. Couple little spots with people still in them. At least three I know of, could be more. The University has some folks, another bunch set up in Victoria

Park, took advantage of the terrain. Another group in an apartment building. I think it was Spring St., someplace around there."

"My daughter and her mom were around there."

"Well, that's some good news at least. Seems like people turning in the night might be a bit less likely if your family didn't turn. Maybe you not turning means your daughter didn't too. Course we don't know for sure, just stories. Anyway, stay for dinner, the food is simple, and we ain't got a lot of spices, but it's good stuff. All local grown, we ate all the stuff from the grocery stores months ago."

There was a small menu, a choice of chicken, pork, beef, or fish. Jasper had the roast beef, something he had never expected to eat again. The food was amazing. Jasper wasn't sure if it would have been the best meal ever had he not been so hungry for so long, but it stood a chance at it. The beef was slow cooked and smothered in gravy. There were mashed potatoes with it, drenched in butter. The vegetables were also simple fare, peas, carrots, a bit of corn. It didn't matter, it was all delicious.

They started to get a rundown on the situation on the island. There were a number of settlements. Like Jasper had guessed, the island had come through the zombies better than Nova Scotia by a huge margin. In Nova Scotia, they had run into exactly two other groups, only one of which had a base of operations. PEI had a number of advantages. The low population density and large farming population meant that people lived far apart and tended to have guns. Also, with that much of the land used for farming food security was pretty much guaranteed for the winter. Next year might be more of a challenge, but it was close to harvest when things fell apart, so most of the active work involved with growing was done. The people left just needed to grab and store as much as they could. Generators were common.

Apparently, the bridge defence had gone badly though. The defenders set up the barricades and then got overwhelmed at the Borden-Carleton barricade when a large horde hit them in mid-September. The sentries on the bridge rushed to the rescue and mostly got killed. It was bad planning and bad luck.

Jasper had hope. Despite the delay in getting there, there was a chance that Taylor was still okay. The fact that Charlottetown had surviving communities, one close to her home, cemented that in his head. He was frantic to get going.

They were shown a small guest shack they could stay in. It was crudely built and drafty, but it had a makeshift wood stove and a couple of cots. They also had a bit of candle their hosts had provided them. The electricity was reserved for the main building, although they had strung lights around the fence, to use if they were attacked. They were kept dark the rest of the time.

"Okay," Jasper said, "This is good news. There's a chance, a real chance, that Taylor isn't dead. More than I could have hoped for when I started out."

Naomi sat down on the cot. "Damn. I happy for you, surprised though. Didn't think it was really possible. Man. I think we stay here couple days though. Get our strength up, take no chances."

"Yeah, absolutely. We have managed to get lucky way too many times so far. It's hard though, we're so close now."

"I know, but that don't mean we shouldn't wait. If homegirl is aight she gon' still be a'ight if we wait a minute."

"I know, I know you're right. It's just hard, how do I make myself wait?"

Candice cleared her throat, "Look, um, I love you guys. Really. People say I'd die for you all the time, but I would... you know I would. Here's the thing: I don't know if I can keep going."

"You mean stay here, join the community?"

"Yeah, it might turn out Beth is another snake like Robert, but I don't think so. I think she's a good person. I'm tired. I don't want to abandon you, leave you in the lurch, but I'm so fucking tired."

"Look, you don't owe me anything. In fact, at this point, I owe you, my life at least, and probably the next few lives as well. After what happened with Sasha, Matt, Jordan, even Snow, I don't know how many more people dying on my quest I can deal with. Stay, make a life here. We will find a place in Charlottetown, somewhere with decent people. We'll be in touch, a few months down the line at least we'll know there's other communities out there to trade with."

Naomi gave Candice a hug. "Me, I got Jasper's back girl. Don't even worry bout it. We good aight?"

"Yeah, I'm gonna miss you though."

"I know. Gon' miss you too. Still, all good. Me and Jasper, we be fine."

After, when they got a quiet moment, Jasper said to Naomi, "Thank you. I'm actually glad Candice is staying here. I could use her, but at least she's going to be safe. Don't know if I could have kept going if you'd bailed too though. It's still a long way and going it alone... I don't even want to think about."

"All good. You probably get lost five feet out the front door, I don't go with you."

Jasper and Naomi stayed two days at the Blue Goose settlement and then hit the road. During that time they worked hard on whatever was needed. Jasper also demonstrated making rocket stoves and explained the concept of rocket stove mass heaters. When he left they were in the process of figuring out how to produce enough mass heaters for the entire compound. He also gave them a basic rundown on how to create cob buildings. The labour involved was pretty high, but the benefits for a situation like this were also huge. He was surprised none of them had looked at it, but really it was more of a hippie thing, and the farming community on PEI tends to be more conservative. He only knew about them due to spending so much time studying prepper stuff. As they were leaving Beth handed each of them a heavy machete and said, "Good luck. You are welcome back anytime, both of you. If you do manage to settle in Charlottetown keep us in mind. Might be good to have some other communities, maybe start trying to rebuild something here. The blades are payment for the stoves, so take them. We've got lots more."

The weather was bad, not terrible. Cold drizzle, no snow. They headed down the road, missing the compound as soon as they got outside. The sky was leaden and low. One thing that they had learned at the compound: It was early December. The sixth in fact. This was the first time in months that Jasper had known the date.

The landscape was flat and empty. They passed houses and the wreckage of houses that had burned. PEI might have fared better than Nova Scotia, but that didn't mean everything there was okay. It was in pretty rough shape. Jasper thought that about one in every three houses was a burnt out shell. Zombies were infrequent and easy to spot from a distance.

Their route was picked using info from the community. One of the major factors was that there was an area that was considered dangerous because of a band of bandits, right in the middle of the most direct route. While most of humanity was pulling together, these guys were preying on anyone they could get near. That meant staying near the south shore or moving all the way up to the north shore. They stuck to the south, staying mostly in sight of the water. As they were walking one day, Jasper nudged Naomi and said, "Hey look, fishing boats!"

It was true, a dozen or so small boats were headed out to sea, despite the bitter cold. That particular day the skies were clear and blue, a few wispy clouds high up. Most were motoring, but a couple had crisp, white sails out.

The road passed through rolling fields, broken by the occasional small patch of trees, mostly next to the road. The trees were barren, brown and grey sticks thrust against the emptiness. Most of the fields were covered in crops, unharvested and rotten, decaying on the ground. After the day with the boats, it rained, ceaselessly. Tiny daggers of cold hitting their skin, as much ice as water half the time. The rain kept falling, miserable and damp. It was just the two of them, seemingly alone in the world.

They knew they weren't far. Probably a week or two's journey in this new world. In the old world it would have taken less than an hour. Jasper had a moment of sorrow when he realized that his entire journey, months of it, would have been less than a day before. A long days drive sure, but just a day. It was a drive he had made many, many times in the past. One that nobody would ever make again. The world had shrunk, closed itself off. Jasper had spent some time in Vancouver, he doubted it would be possible to get back there in his lifetime. The journey would take years. This former single days worth of journey had taken more than forty lives, it was hard to imagine the cost of reaching the far side of the country.

They kept pushing, putting in the miles every day. They found shelter in abandoned homes most nights. It might be a few hours walk between homes, but you could usually see the next one from where you were. The roads they were on were small and winding. Often it was easier to cut across the fields, so that's what they did.

Things got tense again around New Dominion. There was a bridge, and Jasper had developed a bad feeling about bridges. He managed to find a vantage point that gave him a clear view of both approaches. PEI is fairly flat, so there wasn't much, but most of the roads do have some trees next to them. He climbed a tree despite the cold freezing his fingers. It had started to snow, light fluffy flakes lazily falling from the sky. The air was still. It was cold, but the kind of cold that feels sheltered and mild. Jasper couldn't see anything near the bridge and he had a clear view of both shores, so they made their way across, as cautiously as they could manage.

The snow was still falling, and it was sticking to the ground. Still, they walked on. Finally, the snow got to be too much. It was building up rapidly, impeding their ability to walk. They had managed to walk past most of the houses, but there was a farm nearby. The house itself was a charred ruin, but the barn appeared to be intact.

The barn doors were closed, however, there was a small side door that was unlocked. They made their way inside. It was cold, frigid stale air. No animals inside, living or dead, and no walking dead either. There was a hayloft with a ladder up to it. The hay was low, clearly, it hadn't been harvested that year, but it wasn't empty.

They formed a little nest out of hay and waited in the chill. The hay was decent insulation, but it was cold enough to see their breath. They huddled together and stayed the night.

The next day dawned crisp and clear. The temperature was low, but high enough that they could see the snow melting. Once enough of it had cleared they started out. The walking was hard, and they were moving even slower than usual. They were close, so very close. A single days walk in the old days. A few minutes drive. It took them days to get in sight of Charlottetown. For the most part, they were able to find places to stay, but the snow kept coming and the roads kept getting worse. The one night there was a storm, one that brought the temperature up. It started to rain, and it kept raining into the next day. The snow cleared, but in its place it left rivers of mud, every puddle turned into a lake, every ditch a raging torrent. Everything started to flood. There were places where the road vanished under fast flowing water.

Finally, they saw the city. The road into town went over a low bridge, and right now that low bridge was two feet under water. They had no way across where they were. Jasper knew they could get around the river heading west, although it added even more time to the journey. Resigned they set out again. Jasper wished for snow shoes, a truck with a high wheel base, a boat, anything.

Can't Rely on Anybody

Standing in the suburb on the south shore Robert could see the city proper across the river, low buildings and houses. Charlottetown had never been very built up, he guessed it never would be now. In between him and the city was a small island with a shopping complex, nothing else. A couple of zombies wandered between the shops, aimless and confused. Not enough to worry him. The shopping complex was exactly what he was looking for, a place he could ambush Jasper and his people, maybe even find some relative comfort. The river might not be the best water in the world, but he was confident that if he boiled it they would be fine.

As they walked through the shops they started to attract a following. More and more zombies were heading toward them, coming from both sides of the river. Robert found an open door in the shopping complex. It was a Reebok store. Apparently, they weren't the first to shelter there. Inside there was clear evidence of people, but it looked old, like maybe someone had sheltered there months ago, and it had been empty for a long time since. The large glass doors had rough cloth hung over them, as did the large window. The glass was still intact, and the window had a steel cage covering it. Robert locked the door once he got inside.

A little human nest had been built out of coats and other clothing, most of the items of clothing still had tags on them. There was a door at the back of the retail area, again not locked. Robert went through and found a stock room with a set of stairs at the far end. Robert went up, nerves on edge. The stairwell was dark, just a hint of light peeking around the edge of the door at the top. He made it to the door, listened, ear pressed to the thin wood veneer of the hollow core door. When he didn't hear anything he opened the door, slowly, cautiously. The space was a hallway, cloaked in shadows, a small window at one end letting in grey winter light. There were doors on either side, one was slightly ajar, dim light leaking around the edges. Robert went for that one first, since any zombies would have likely already made it out to the hall, meaning it was far more likely to be empty. Inside was a small staff lounge. It was comfortable a comfortable space, lots of sleek black furniture including some couches. Robert guessed whoever had made the nest downstairs hadn't made it up here. There was also a large window. He looked out and realized that where he was was even better than he had thought in terms of setting a trap. The island had roads leading on and off, but the island itself was just the shopping complex. A narrow channel that offered no cover and no alternate routes this time of year. Swimming was not a viable option in December. He would have a clear shot at Jasper from the moment he came in view.

The one thing that was a problem was heat. Robert scouted the ground floor, leaving Mona and Trevor in the employee lounge. Mona was useless, too weak to do much of anything except provide for his needs, sometimes he wondered if liberating a fleshlight from one of the stores would be just as good, and Trevor needed to guard her, make sure she was safe for him. He found an entry to the next store and the next. Apparently, they were all connected inside, a series of passages at the back of buildings. Most of the doors were locked, but a solid kick changed that. Near the centre, there was a set of stairs leading down to a basement. It was clean and dry, and there was a gas generator, shiny and new. He fired it up. The lights came on around him.

He made his way back to where he had left Mona and Trevor. As soon as the lights came on they had tried the sink. The taps were working. Best of all, after a few minutes, the water started to flow hot. Mona was naked, scrubbing her emaciated frame with a dripping cloth. Robert took a moment to appreciate her body, maybe she was better than a fleshlight after all.

They spent days there, getting cleaned up, gleaning food from the stores around them. There was nothing fresh of course, but there was a restaurant in the complex, with plenty of canned food. The stoves didn't work, probably out of propane, but they had a microwave and a toaster oven in the upstairs staff room, an electric kettle. It was better than they had lived in a long time.

Things went bad after the rain started. It was pounding down, tropical force, but cold - barely above freezing. Enough above to melt the snow though, the river was rising fast.

Robert spent most of his time looking out the window at the south shore, scanning with his rifle scope. He didn't want to take a chance on missing Jasper. Finally one day his diligence paid off. He spotted Jasper, Naomi following close behind. Apparently the bitch had survived too. At least it was just the two of them. The rain made vision hard. He saw them approach the bridge, just out of the range he could manage in that weather. He saw them turn, he saw them walk the other way. He had no way of following them. There were no good vantage points in the direction they headed, and he didn't know their route anymore. He scanned the ground and realized why they had turned. Fuck. The river was now above the bridges, flooding over the ground. It would be minutes at most before the basement started to flood. No more lights, no more hot water.

The only bright side was that the approaching zombies were washed away. It was a short trip to the ocean, and they were headed that way quickly. Provided the water receded soon they would be okay. Sure, the comfort was over, but it was nothing worse than they had endured so far... and sure enough at that moment the generator failed. The room was cast into half-light, the rain beating down on the roof.

It took a while for the place to get cold. They had moved some of the coats and stuff upstairs to use as blankets. They huddled under the mounds of coats most of the time, exhausting their meager supplies. The waters finally stopped rising after 3 more days. The flooding was 4 feet deep downstairs, and the building was showing signs of strain. Tree branches kept washing past. By day 5 the water was only ankle deep. The bridge to the south was washed away, but the one into Charlottetown proper was still mostly intact.

Robert thought to himself "Well, nothing for it now. Just find a spot to set myself up. Deal with Jasper if I see him."

It was probably the most rational thought he had had in months, although he didn't realize it.

The journey into town was hard. Charlottetown was the most heavily populated place on Prince Edward Island, and that meant it was the most zombie heavy place as well. Surprisingly though, the numbers weren't all that high. Sure, there were clusters, but Robert and company discovered that by moving cautiously they were largely able to avoid them. The odd individual zombie didn't prove to be much of a challenge.

They traveled through low density neighbourhoods, made up of single family homes. It seemed like that was pretty much what Charlottetown consisted of. It wasn't that the zombies were no threat, they were still around, still trying to kill them. It was more that so long as they kept moving the numbers were low enough that they were able to stay ahead of them. Robert knew however that even he would run out of physical reserves eventually and the zombies wouldn't. The zombies would win unless he figured something out. Mona and Trevor were already starting to flag.

One downside to Charlottetown: single family homes didn't make for great fortresses. They needed someplace that could be secured. They passed a couple of hotels. The first one looked like a no go, there were dozens of zombies clustered inside the front door, trying to break it down, trying to get out. Somebody had jammed a bunch of junk in front of the door, which was preventing it from opening. It was straining under the weight of the bodies trying to push through it. Robert didn't want to be there when it finally gave, so he continued on. The next one only had a couple of zombies visible in the lobby. The door wasn't locked, which probably accounted for it. The undead had pushed against the door and had managed to get out, in fact that was happening again, with the two that were left.

Robert took out Jasper's sword. He didn't have the smaller man's skill with it, but he was getting better fast. One of the zombies was a Japanese tourist, fulfilling the stereotypes nicely by having no less than three cameras hung around his neck. Robert took his head off with a clean blow and turned to the other one. A hotel maid by the look of things. She was badly decayed, her face and body showed many, many bite marks. Robert closed and thrust his sword into her open mouth, aiming slightly up. The resemblance to fellatio excited him, and then the tip of the blade came through the back of her head and she fell to the ground, limp and finally motionless. Mona and Trevor rushed to follow him into the hotel.

A few zombies followed, but they couldn't figure out how to pull the door open, so they were pushing against the frame.

The inside of the hotel was cold. The place hadn't been heated in a long time. This wasn't going to work long term, but for now it was okay, if they could get enough heat going.

Robert checked the cubbies behind the counter, looking for unoccupied rooms. The place had been doing a decent business over the summer, a lot of the keys were gone. It seemed likely that many of the rooms would still have guests in them, but there were a few vacant. He picked one on the second floor and headed up to it.

The lock was of course not working, a safety feature if the power went out, but the door was latched and when he entered the room it was empty. Cold as hell, but empty.

The next priority was warmth. He left Trevor and Mona in the room, wrapped in blankets, and went in search of something he could make a fire in. Eventually he found a large steel drum in the furnace room, near a bunch of loose cinder blocks. If they were careful it was possible they wouldn't burn down the hotel. The smoke would be a problem of course, but so long as they left the window open a bit they could vent some of the smoke outside.

It worked better in theory than in practice, but it did work. In the end they took the mattresses off the beds and put them on the floor, throwing the beds out of the room. That way they were under the worst of the smoke and could still breathe. It wasn't going to last them long, but it was a place to recoup their energy and start to plan. There were maps of the city in the lobby as well.

Robert thought the golf club was his best option, but he would have to see conditions on the ground. There were very few apartment buildings, and one of those might make a decent spot as well. There were also a number of options downtown.

One last blessing. There was a fair bit of canned food in the kitchen. The hotel was set up to serve a large number of people, so it was enough even just in tins for them to eat well for an extended period.

I'm Living Downtown

"Fuck. Days. We are losing days getting around this shit." Jasper was frustrated by the delay once again. It seemed like every time they found a path into the city flooding was stopping them in their tracks.

"Nothing we can do. Just keep walking. You know we gonna make it. River don't give a shit you wanna go faster." Naomi was patient. To her, it was all very much the same. She was sticking with Jasper out of loyalty and had no hopes for Charlottetown over any other place. The small city seemed viable, lots of forage around, lots of empty homes, nothing else really to recommend it though. It was a small and poor place, all small buildings.

They finally reached the city, ragged and tired. The first houses started to show up. Again, many of them had burnt. You could see whole swaths where one house had caught fire and the flames had leapt to the next house. The signs of civilization being wiped from the face of the planet. Jasper wanted to make it to the downtown core. Karen had been living with her boyfriend on Spring Park Road. They were going to need to rest before then, to recoup some strength. Too many dead between them and downtown.

They found a small farm, within the city limits. It was, however, a working farm. There were cattle in the field, looking somewhat worse for wear, but alive. The farmhouse was in good repair. They opened the door and met the owner, an elderly man wearing nothing but a pair of boxers, body blackened with blood pooling and rot, guts protruding over his boxers, stained with shit and piss. His smell settled around them, turning the air thick. They say you can get used to anything, but if there was one thing that Jasper hadn't managed to get used to about this new world it was the smells. Sweet rotten meat mixed with human waste followed the zombies wherever they went, building a miasma of stench that was almost solid, almost a thing you could touch. The smell pervaded his senses, bringing him to the edge of vomiting. The cold, clear late fall air and small number of zombies had left him unused to the stench again. He drew his machete and smashed through the old man's skull.

Inside they found what had ripped the man's face apart. There were two dogs, starved to death from the look of it. Lying in the living room, rotted and decayed. Jasper didn't want to stay there. "I can't. Too much. I can't stay here."

"I know honey, but you gonna. This ain't Snow. Now, grab the other end of this rug. Let's get them bundled up and out of here."

Jasper pulled himself together and did as Naomi said, the two of them hauling the remains of the dogs outside.

They build a fire in the stove and raided the kitchen. As usual for a farmhouse, there were preserves and lots of canned food. Having the wood stove to cook on made a huge difference, as did the oil lantern that was hanging in the kitchen. If there's one thing an Islander is used to, it's power outages.

Jasper started packing canned food into his bag. "Okay, so let's grab what we can, head out."

"Hell no. You can barely stand up white boy, and I ain't carrying your ass. We staying here until we get a rest. Taylor still alive right now, she still be alive in two days. Don't be fucking stupid."

"Shit, I just, I'm so close now. I don't know how to wait anymore. I'm sorry." Jasper broke down into tears, big gaping sobs, unable to catch his breath. Naomi put her arms around him and held him until the tears subsided.

They spent two days in the farm house. The house was set up with grates leading from the living room into the other rooms, a way for the wood stove to heat everything, and some of the rooms also had fireplaces. This house had stood long before central heating became available. They slept in comfort their two nights there. Jasper was never able to get the dogs out of his mind though.

Finally, they gathered up everything they could and left, headed for downtown.

Jasper knew that one of the places with a community was an apartment building on the corner of Spring Park. He thought that was the best starting place, because of how close it was to where Karen had lived before the collapse. Spring Park meant making their way into the most densely populated part of the city, but densely populated was a relative term. As they walked Jasper said, "Does it seem like there should be more zombies to you?"

"Yeah, now shut up about it. We don't want to tempt fate. I'd say knock on wood, but we probably get 50 fucking zombies running over cause they heard it."

"Good point. Still, though, this place was decent sized. Over a hundred thousand I think. The flood probably helped a bit. We better keep a good eye out though."

They passed subdivisions, and then neighbourhoods, and then the university. Naomi pointed to the university grounds. "Smoke. Just a bit though."

"Looks like a cooking fire. Probably we have survivors there. That's amazing! Survivors! Wanna go check it out?"

"Was thinking yeah, but zombies between us and them, lots of them. Maybe we skip it, come back once we find your brat."

"Sounds like a plan. Still, people alive! Amazing news. If the building turns out to be inhabited that's two groups just in this city."

Downtown was denser, there were zombies wandering the streets. Jasper and Naomi moved from cover to cover, travelling through back yards where possible. Back yards meant fences, and that meant they could climb, while the zombies would be stopped. Normally it would be an hour or so from where they were to Spring Park. The hours walk took them a day and a half. Eventually, they could see the building. It was surrounded by zombies, but they saw smoke coming from the chimney, and there were other signs that this was a place inhabited by humans. The parking lot was now fenced in, with high barricades. There were stakes driven into the ground, pointed out. Many of the stakes had zombies impaled on them, still trying to pull themselves forward despite the damage it was doing to their bodies. There were also long ropes leading across the street to many of the surrounding houses. All of the ground floor windows were boarded up, although the windows on the upper floors seemed fine.

By Charlottetown standards this building was large, but by any other standard, it was tiny. The thing took up one street on a short block and was only three stories tall. Jasper was trying to figure out how to get to the building then the problem solved itself. Someone came out on the roof and yelled down to him, "Hey, get up on the roof over there if you want to come in."

The figure was pointing to one of the houses across the street. Jasper and Naomi headed for the house, moving fast. A few of the zombies had noticed them, but only a few. Most of them were still fixated on the building. They headed inside and up to the roof. There was a line running from the building to the house, but once they got close it was clear it was a very, very thick length of aircraft cable, doubled on itself. Kind of like a clothes line. There were handles that could clip on to the cable and had a loop of padded wire hanging off of them, to allow someone to sit in them. The person on the roof yelled, "Get one of the loops around your butt, we'll pull you over."

Jasper got himself seated in one of the loops, Naomi took the next one. They needed both hands on the handle part to stay stable, and they were basically helpless the entire time they were being pulled across. It was friendly, easy, and a death trap if the people in the building wanted it to be. The cable started pulling them across, high above the heads of the zombies.

There was a group on top of the building. Six large men dressed in camo gear and layered rags. They looked happy, smiles on all their faces, but they were heavily armed. All of them had ragged beards. The loop left Jasper suspended about six feet above the roof, and he still needed his hands to steady himself. If he let go he started spinning. There was no easy way down. The group of men brought a wheeled platform close and then started asking them questions. He cut them off by saying, "Hey, you guys know Karen Smith and Taylor Pellerine?"

"How you know them?" one of the men asked.

"I'm Taylor's dad. Karen's my ex."

"Well shit, that's crazy. Taylor's going to flip. Hell, even Karen might be happy. Let's get you guys down! Jed, go get Taylor and Karen."

They waited. Jasper was so amped up he couldn't keep still. He explained their journey to the men, but kept bouncing up on his feet, excitement bubbling out of every pore. Everyone seemed to be catching Jasper's joy, even Naomi was hyped up, talking fast, words bubbling out at a million miles an hour.

Taylor came bursting out of the rooftop doorway, a bundle of thirteen-year-old energy. She was still half little girl, dressed in cast off clothing. Her face still had a bit of baby fat. In the months since Jasper had seen her, she had grown up a lot. Her dark hair was cut short and her face was dirty. She took a running jump and landed in Jasper's arms, knocking him over. He didn't mind at all. He hugged her, holding her close to him. All this way, and finally, finally, he had found her. Karen came up a little slower, a little more reserved. It made sense, after all, she was his ex. They didn't hate each other, but the divorce had been hard. At that moment Jasper didn't care at all.

Naomi stuck out a hand "Hey, I'm Naomi. Been walking with Jasper since just past the airport. Sorry, it took a minute to get here."

"Hey, I'm Karen. The hyperactive teenager wrapping herself around your... friend is Taylor ."

"Figured. She's just like he said. So glad you alive, both of you!" Naomi replied.

Karen gave Jasper an obvious look as she met Naomi. Right, that was part of why they broke up, the jealousy. No way she could know that Jasper saw Naomi as, if not quite a sister, maybe something even closer than that, a comrade in arms. Any chance of them hooking up had evaporated hundreds of kilometres back down the road. Karen looked good for the circumstances, not as thin as she might have looked, less weather worn, like she had survived the apocalypse relatively unscathed. "Did Pete make it?"

Pete was Karen's boyfriend, the reason she had moved to the island.

"No. He turned that first morning. Taylor and I had to run. I was up doing my Pilates when it happened."

"Lucky. If you'd been asleep... I don't want to think about it."

They talked, each giving their stories. Karen's was a lot less harsh than Jasper's. Taylor cried when she heard that Snow had died, and even more when she heard how. Jasper tried to minimize it, but it was still too raw for him. Karen introduced Jasper to the people in the building, and explained more or less how things worked. The setup was pretty secure, but it had weak points. Nothing a zombie could easily overwhelm, but in enough numbers they could be an issue.

The building had annexed the rest of the block, and was planning on converting the backyards into crop land, and the houses into additional quarters. The whole thing was low key, and ambitious in a minimal sort of way. They had drawn up plans to take over the surrounding blocks over time, piece by piece. Each block had to be secured and then access built to bring it into the fold. Their overall plan was a series of cells, each one linked to the others, but with gates that could close. That way if there was a breach, if the zombies did get in, it would be limited in impact. Apparently someone in planning had watched zombie movies too.

The building had some electricity even, although it was pretty limited. A bank of solar panels on neighbouring roofs, some lead acid batteries pulled from cars and set up down in the basement. It meant they were able to run a few freezers to keep some frozen food available, and keep the furnace pumps going.

It was a pretty loose community. The people all came from different backgrounds, different lifestyles, etc. They didn't even get along all that well. Didn't really matter. They had one guy, a young student from the college who lived in the building, John. He was the closest thing they had to a leader, despite only being in his early twenties. He had set up the solar collection, the idea of the cells, the winch system. Apparently he was very unhappy with the rear parking lot. It had a single sliding gate they had set up, and he was trying to figure out some other system, something more secure. For the most part they didn't use it, but if a foraging party brought back something large it would need to open, and that was weak point for the building. The working plan was to set up kind of an airlock, fence either end of the block the parking lot was on, and between the houses across the street. That would allow them to get large items in and the dispatch any zombies that followed in a controlled manner, before opening the final gate and letting the load in. Problem was the weather had turned, and they needed the materials and manpower to do it.

Other than that, the building was well supplied with food. They had a full cow in the freezers, lots of frozen vegetables, lots of canned food. Someone had raided a supermarket and managed to get a full refrigerated truck into the lot two days after first night, and it was enough that they were still living off of it.

Jasper had seen a few viable communities in his travels, but this was the first he had seen in a city. It showed that it was possible, that abandoning cities wasn't something that needed to happen. Humanity could continue its pattern of building specialization into society, lots of people with different skill sets doing different jobs. He felt in that moment like they were going to make it.

Reap What You Sow

Robert saw the settlement as he wandered the city. It was obvious it was there, all the zombies clustered around it. Clearly, there were humans inside. He spotted Jasper about a second later. The snake was being carried over the road on a wire. Fucking bastard, polluting another place with his chaos and anarchy.

Discipline. That was what was needed. Jasper had no real discipline. This place looked like it was in the same boat. If humanity was going to survive this anarchy needed to be stamped out. Chain of command needed to be sacrosanct. The more he looked at the place the more convinced he was that it was just wrong. Sure, it might last for a little while - and while it did people would be seduced. Anarchy is fun, it allows you to be a child, to think like a child. To be a real adult though, you need rules and order, and you need to accept them completely. People can't be trusted to live how they want. Increasingly he was convinced that places like this needed to die so that the species could live. So he watched, and he waited. He had food, a nearby house with a decent vantage point, Trevor and Mona to make sure that food was prepped and ready. He studied the building. People came and went at all hours. Nobody really seemed to be in charge. He also spotted the weak points, lots and lots of them. Clear evidence that these people were inherently weak, that that trait flowed from them to their preparations. Better to have a few people who knew the chain of command, what to do, than to have a large number in chaos.

He was going to take the gate down, make this place end. Sure, some people would die... that would happen eventually anyway. They couldn't be allowed to infect everyone with their ways. Humanity needed to survive. The question was how to get the gate taken care of, and how to make sure the building door was open after he did. He didn't think the second part of that question would be hard... just run up and open it. The gate itself though, a bit more of a challenge. He remembered passing a Canadian Tire a ways back. There would be things he could use to make explosives. Enough to take out the gate at least. Once this place was gone the next place could be made better, order could be preserved.

In the Mouth of Madness

Mona had recognized that Robert had lost his mind a long time ago. She'd been around enough mentally ill people to know what it looked like. This was clearly insanity. Doing something about it was a different matter. He was bigger, stronger, had a mean right hook. A mean temper too. She was good in a fight, but he outweighed her by at least a hundred pounds... she had to go along with him. She was terrified. Everything about herself that had come back while travelling with Jasper had died since that day in the camp. Every time Robert smashed her in the face or the stomach she went back to the little girl she had been, the one in the trailer park whose mother had terrorized her, beaten her randomly because she wanted to. The only thing she had to protect herself was sex. If she fucked Robert, if she did it well, he would be calm, at least briefly. Also, he was good at it. Made her cum, again and again, every time. It was the only respite though, the only source of peace. It brought her right back to trading her body for meth, or booze before that.

She wished she had the strength to stop him, the courage to run away, something. Instead, she took it.

Trevor also seemed broken. The young soldier was never very smart, or good with people... but he at least had a light in his eyes once. Now he didn't. He barely ever spoke, just replied when Robert asked a question, usually with a single word. He followed orders unthinkingly, like a robot. Between Robert and the road, Trevor was no longer present, had nothing left inside. Mona could tell. She had seen guys like him before. People who just stopped being people with enough abuse. Sometimes she wondered if someone else would see her like that. Most of the time she assumed they would.

Robert left. Mona knew she should warn the building, warn Jasper and Naomi, about what was coming. There was nobody in the world who had ever been kinder to her. She just couldn't make herself do it. What if Trevor decided to stop her? What if Robert came back and she was still outside? She waited, perched on the edge of indecision, stuck between knowing what she wanted, what she should do, and the fear. In the end, the fear won. She lay down curled up in a ball and hoped that she would die before Robert got back.

She didn't. He returned with a bunch of bottles and things and went into the bathroom, muttering to himself. His once handsome face was now a mass of sores and dirt, she didn't think he knew. He'd been picking at his own skin for a while, probably a reaction to the constant filth that was his new normal state. His beard was long and unkempt. She was pretty sure he had fleas, then again so did she, the itch was contributing to her breakdown.

She waited, lying there in the half light, listening to his muttering, smelling the acrid chemical smells. Trevor was keeping watch on the door, making sure nobody, living or otherwise, came in to interrupt them.

Mona started crying, making sure to stay silent, so Robert didn't hear her.

I Love It When a Plan Comes Together

Robert had his explosives. Not exactly what he wanted, not military grade or anything, but enough to take out that shitty gate. He waited for the cover of darkness. No point in making his life harder and alerting the building. Discipline. No matter how much he wanted to move he had to wait.

Darkness fell, the days were short now. He moved, stealthily, trying not to attract the zombies on the street too early. He wanted their attention when the gate went, but he wanted to make sure they gave him time to plant the explosives. For some reason, they seemed to be paying less attention to him than usual.

He made it to the gate without getting noticed. Then he set the explosives on either side of the gate, enough that it would fall, and would get some attention. Mona and Trevor were waiting back in the house, as they should be. They were weak. Would only hold him back for something like this.

The fuses on his explosives were short, a minute or so at most. He lit them and moved back. A zombie grabbed him from behind, drawn to his movement. He flipped the creature, a classic judo throw, and slammed a knife into its brain. He lay prone as the spark hit the end of the fuse. The delay was only a second or so, and then the explosives blew. There was a brief bright flash and a muted sound. The shockwave rolled over him, a feeling of pressure, there and then gone. He popped up and ran, straight through where the gate used to be.

The rear door was mostly glass. It was closed and locked, but it was still just glass. Robert fired two shots into it, then smashed it with the butt of his gun. The glass shattered and collapsed. The dirty anarchists were now open to the zombies. That weak point had proved to be one they couldn't afford.

By now people were coming, running down the stair towards him. He ducked back into the night, slipping the crowd of zombies who were coming in. There were hundreds of them, more every minute.

He slipped along the wall of the building and found himself a narrow alcove to hide in. It wasn't much protection, but it was enough. By maintaining strict discipline and not moving or making a noise he would blend into the wall, the zombies would never see him.

As the defenders streamed down and out, firing on the zombies as they went, Robert scanned their faces... looking for Jasper or Naomi. After a few minutes, he saw the devil, swinging a machete he had acquired somewhere. No need to look for the whore, she could be dealt with after. It was clear the weapon didn't have the versatility and capability of the sword he used to carry, but it was a sharp piece of steel and Jasper seemed to be content with it. Behind him was a woman Robert didn't recognize. Pretty in an intense kind of way, she looked softer and better fed than he was used to these days. Clearly, this woman hadn't been through the same kind of things that he had.

Then Robert spotted the girl. Small and slight, she looked like she was in her early teens. Yet more proof that Jasper was the devil. His child was still alive, while both of Robert's had turned right away. Not that Robert really cared, but it would have been nice to have someone to carry on his legacy. Certainly, his genes were much more valuable than Jasper's.

He waited, looking for an opportunity. The defenders were being overrun, the sheer weight of zombies too much for their limited weapons and training. A bunch of them weren't even fighting. Instead, they were clustered around a dumpster, trying to push it or something. Fucking idiots, don't they know you deal with the immediate threat then worry about other things?

Finally, Jasper was in a clear spot. Robert ran out of his alcove, slamming Jasper with his shoulder, screaming, a wordless cry of rage, as he raised Jasper's sword above his head to bring down on the demon.

Jasper spun on the ground, rolling with the fall and turning as he came up, moving to one side. The heavy blade bit into the concrete.

Jasper kicked out with his right leg, catching Robert just above the left wrist. Robert let the sword go, dropping into a low stance as it fell.

What She Saw in the Night

Naomi ran outside, close behind Jasper. She got separated from him in seconds, turned around and isolated. She was in the open, surrounded by zombies, no cover close at hand. She charged, head down. She thought she was running for the building but wasn't sure. It was loud, gunfire going off on all sides, zombies moaning, impeding her vision. Hands grabbed her, trying to bear her to the ground. She lashed out with her machete, catching dead flesh, one of the arms that was grabbing her came away from its body, fell to the ground. It gave her enough momentum to hit the accelerator inside her, she slammed into a wall, hard. At least she could keep her back to it now.

Naomi turned, pushing hands off of her. She had on light armour, skateboard pads and paintball gear, but it was enough to have kept her alive so far. She swung the machete over and over again, the weight of zombies never seeming to get smaller, until suddenly it did. She found herself in the middle of a calm moment, the eye of the storm so to speak. Where she was there was a slight rise in the ground. She could see most of the battle, clusters of violence swirling around her.

Taylor swung into view, swinging a stick, one end sharpened into a vicious point. Taylor was using her small size and agility to weave back and forth between the zombie. Naomi saw her whirling the stick around, slamming into one zombie after another. They fell, lifeless and limp, but more kept coming. Naomi called out "Taylor, over here!" but the girl didn't hear her.

More and more zombies were piling on to Taylor, cutting her off from the rest of the defenders. One of them grabbed her arm, trying to bite through the armour there. She pushed it off, darted through their legs on the ground and dove into one of the dumpsters lining the lot. She was closer to other defenders now, they were pushing the two dumpsters across the open gate. Her leap moved it the final inches into place, then the lid dropped on her, taking her from Naomi's view.

Naomi could see Karen now too. Karen had a length of re-bar in her hands and was fighting like a demon. More zombies closed on Naomi, she had to fight again herself, her arms starting to fail, to lose strength. If not for the slight armour she would have fallen some time ago.

She drew her arm back and dropped the heavy blade on the skull of a young woman, probably her age when she turned. A pretty redhead, dressed like Ann of Green Gables. The woman fell, and Naomi had another brief gap. She saw a woman, almost a zombie herself, slipping into the compound. Fuck, it was Mona!

Mona was lost to sight instantly, walking between zombies. They didn't seem to even notice her, like she was one of them, but she wasn't moving like them, striding tall and purposeful.

Back to Karen. Karen had her back against another defender, one of the large men with the beards. They were laying out zombies all around them, dozens on the ground. The man slipped, Naomi couldn't see on what, and hit the ground. Zombies piled on him, tearing him to pieces. Naomi felt so helpless, stuck against the wall, no way to make it to Karen. More zombies were coming at her anyway, Karen would have to fend for herself.

When Naomi got her next brief window she saw that the gap in the fence was closed, the flood of zombies stemmed. The two dumpsters weren't enough to close it completely, but they were close enough that the zombies had to try and make it in single file, squeezing through a too narrow gap. A couple of defenders were slamming knives into their skulls as they passed the gap. It was going to be tight, but they stood a chance now.

Naomi scanned for Karen, trying to spot her in the confusion. Finally, she saw her, still fighting, still swinging her piece of re-bar. She wasn't even raising it over her head anymore, slamming zombies in the chest, then pushing the re-bar through their skulls once they fell down, leaning her weight into the bar, it looked like she didn't have the strength left to lift the bar.

Finally one of the zombies grabbed her from behind. Naomi watched her spin, trying to make it around to hit the zombie, but she didn't have the energy left, the strength. The zombie bit deep into her throat, arterial spray washing over the rest of the zombies. They tore her apart, a dozen of them biting into her. The defenders took advantage of the lull, closing on the zombies and dispatching them.

In the far distance something was happening that looked different. Was that Robert? Yes, and that was Jasper at his feet. Naomi abandoned her relatively safe perch, running for them as fast as she could.

Everybody was Kung Fu Fighting

It was quickly obvious that Robert had a major advantage in terms of size and strength. His reach was much longer than Jasper's and his hits were incredibly powerful. Jasper was quicker, more agile. It wasn't obvious to Robert, but Jasper also had a lot more training in unarmed combat. Robert had always relied on being bigger and stronger, and it made him lazy in training. If he could win the combat every time, without having to work too hard, he was clearly doing it right. Jasper on the other hand, while still being a decent sized guy, was not always the biggest, the tallest, the fastest. He made up for it with training and dedication. His shots were precise, and he was more aware, paying more attention to the environment, constantly scanning for any opening, any slight mistake on Robert's part. That's why he was the one who noticed the zombie closing on Robert. The creature grabbed Robert by the arm as he drew his fist back to punch. Robert spun, slamming his huge fist into the creature, sending it flying back. As he did that he felt rabbit punches slamming into his kidney. Robert turned back as Jasper swung a low roundhouse kick into his thigh. It hurt, it hurt a lot. Robert grabbed the smaller man and pulled him off his feet. Technique counts for a lot, but it has limits. He lifted Jasper and threw him to the ground. Jasper hit the pavement, hard.

Robert casually walked two steps and slammed his foot into Jasper's ribs. He heard a crunching sound and Jasper gasped in pain. Jasper was on the edge of blacking out, the pain in his side was so intense. He rolled and fetched up at the feet of a zombie. The creature bent down to grab him. Jasper reached up, shifted his weight, dropping the already unbalanced zombie, sending it crashing to the ground between him and Robert, just as the big man brought his foot down, hard. Robert ended up smashing the zombie, missing Jasper. The zombie tried to bite Robert's leg, forcing Robert to deal with it. Robert slammed his other foot down on the zombies head over and over again until its skull shattered. Jasper's ribs were screaming bands of pain, breathing was fire. He managed to stay conscious, but every movement took him right back to the edge.

Jasper was doing everything he could to stay out of Robert's grasp. He couldn't find the space to get back to his feet. If he wasn't hurt, maybe... but with his ribs damaged as they were, he didn't have a chance. The zombies kept reaching for him, Robert kept pressing forward. Jasper kept moving, rolling, crawling. At one point he was certain Robert had him, but he managed to slide between two zombies, they turned to him and Robert smashed through them, sending them falling to the ground.

There were no zombies around them anymore, just the two of them, a pocket of violence in the calming sea. No more distractions, no more places to hide. Just the two of them, like it was always going to be.

Jasper couldn't lose the big man, couldn't get free, this was it. All this time, all this distance, and he was going to be beaten to death in a parking lot by a madman. At least he'd had a chance to find Taylor, to tell her he loved her. That was something, more than he had expected when he started the journey. His vision started to go black at the edges, his body finally giving up, finally losing the ability to stay conscious.

Just as he blacked out he saw something, a shape from a nightmare closing behind Robert, then the world went away.

Into the Fire

For a long time, Mona just lay there. Trevor was watching to make sure the zombies didn't come in, and maybe to make sure she didn't go out, she wasn't sure. She was curled up on the floor again. Finally, something in her head snapped. If Robert won, if he managed to do whatever mad thing he was trying to do this time, this was the rest of her life. Better to die than that.

She got up and walked to the bathroom. She opened the door, half thinking she was going to get cleaned up, maybe try to look like a human again, when the smell of chemicals hit her. The bathroom wasn't going to work. She closed the door and went downstairs. Trevor looked at her, his eyes dead and empty, then looked back outside. She didn't know if he would let her go or not, or if he would even care at this point. He was already dead, but his body hadn't figured it out yet.

She walked into the kitchen and grabbed a knife. A large chef's knife. It was a high-end blade, she didn't know that, if she had she wouldn't have cared. She just knew that it felt heavy and solid in her hand, something she could use.

Trevor barely looked at her as she approached him. As she walked out the door he said, "Planning to kill him?"

"Yep".

"Good luck".

At that moment there was an explosion, a second later a couple of gunshots. Mona walked down the front stairs. Much to her surprise, Trevor covered her, firing round after round into the zombies. Their attention was split, a bunch headed towards the explosion, but some started swarming the house. Mona saw Trevor take his handgun and place the barrel in his mouth. He pulled the trigger just as the first zombies made it through the door. His body had finally caught up to his spirit.

Mona walked through the zombies. They seemed to ignore her. One or two turned their heads to her, but they turned away without touching her. As she walked the zombies became denser, but she was able to slip through them. Finally, she slipped into the parking lot. Humans were fighting off the zombies, and thankfully they seemed to be winning. Mona had known that Robert had lost it, but to purposefully try to sacrifice humans to the zombies was far, far worse than she had believed even he was capable of. Sure, he was a sadistic brute, but this was monstrous evil, almost cartoonish evil.

She scanned the crowd, looking for Robert. Finally, she spotted him, beating someone who lay on the ground. Robert seemed to share whatever it was that was making the zombies ignore her. Maybe they were both dead inside. One or two seemed to notice him, briefly, but most were oblivious to his presence, almost as if he was one of them. Nobody else had that advantage. The guy on the ground was dodging the zombies, moving aside as they lunged at him. He was in trouble. It took her a minute to realize that it was Jasper. Robert's obsession had driven him to this.

She skirted through the combat, moving purposefully. One of the zombies did pay attention to her, finally, reaching for her. She responded the way she usually did to physical threats, Robert notwithstanding, and slammed her blade into the creature's temple. It fell, instantly.

Mona had always been good in a fight. A combination of fast reflexes and having no limits. Robert was different of course, he was so much larger than her, and even more savage than she was, he took her strength away. Against most people and things though, she was a killer.

Finally, she got near, as Robert pulled a handgun. He was aiming it at Jasper. There were almost no zombies left, the last few were being mopped up. Jasper was unconscious on the pavement. Robert's first shot went wide, slamming into the pavement. His hand was trembling, body shaking with rage and adrenaline.

Robert lined up the shot again. Mona struck. She slammed the kitchen knife into his side, below his rib cage. He grunted in surprise and turned. They locked eyes and Mona could see the madness, the rage, the fire. Robert dropped his gun and grabbed her throat. She stabbed him again, in the stomach, and again, and again. The world started to go dark around the edges... she could see that the zombies were noticing them, and then that Robert was one of the zombies, the colour draining from his eyes. Her last thought before he tore her apart was "I got you motherfucker. I win".

Barbarians at the Gate

Jasper got up, trying to process what he had seen. He grabbed his sword from where Robert had dropped it, and turned, ready to keep fighting if he had to. He could barely breathe. The lot seemed nearly empty, with all the zombies down. Robert was already down, a nice neat bullet hole in his forehead. Mona was just getting up, her eyes white and full of hunger. Where the hell had she come from? Jasper swung the sword, taking her head off. He cried a little as he did it. The pain in his side was beyond anything he could imagine. He didn't know how he was able to stand.

Jasper started looking for Taylor, scanning the faces around him. Naomi came running, grabbed him under the shoulder, apparently she could see that he was in too much pain to stand on his own.

"Taylor, she jumped in the dumpster. She's alright. Let's go get your girl."

Naomi supported him as they made their way across the parking lot. Amazing how small it actually was, space for a couple dozen cars at most. So much had happened, a war, in a few thousand square feet. Jasper thought his monstrous house in Bedford was larger.

Jasper said, "I have to stand on my own, I have to make sure Taylor sees me standing strong."

"Kay jackass. All good, but you sure you ain't gonna drop soon as I let you go though?"

"Yep. Well, maybe sure is pushing it. How about let's try it and if I fall down we go another route?"

Naomi let go, and Jasper didn't fall down. It was a close thing though. He let Naomi take care of opening the dumpster lid, he didn't think he could manage it on his own.

Taylor looked up at him, tears streaming down her face. She reached out her arms, and he grabbed her, lifting her into an embrace. He almost faltered, almost dropped her, but he didn't. No amount of pain was going to make him let Taylor down now.

They mopped up the zombies pretty quickly from there. As soon as no more could come in it was a matter of time. Jasper sat that part out, his injuries were bad enough that in the old world he would have been in the hospital by now. The building had a doctor of sorts, really a paramedic, but he was the closest thing they had. He patched Jasper up, bound his chest, told him to stay off of his feet. Including Karen, the building lost ten people. Robert and Mona made it an even dozen. Jasper was never sure who put down Robert after he turned, but he didn't really care. He hated the man, of course, but he never developed the same kind of fixation that Robert had on him. Instead, he moved his focus to cleaning up, to making things better for his daughter.

The next few days were hard. They had to repair the damage to the fence, building a new gateway. Naomi spent most of her days pouring over maps, figuring out where supplies might be. There was an intense flurry of activity. Jasper spent a lot of time outside despite the protests of the medic, and of Naomi, but he made sure to spend as much time as possible with Taylor.

They were able to find the supplies, not only to fix the gate but to finally add the extra gates to the ends of the street. They lost three more people during that operation. Construction was hard, always. It was Taylor that came up with the portable building zones. Vehicle mounted temporary fencing that could be interlinked to keep zombies away from the work crews, something they adopted much later on.

As winter progressed the building dug in, hardened their perimeter. They maintained their commitment to allowing new people in, however. More people meant survival.

A note to my readers

This story came from NanoWriMo (http://nanowrimo.org/). The first draft was written in a month. It wasn't hard to manage, a fact which shocked me. That was what set me on this path, re-ignited the passion for writing I had abandoned many years earlier.

If you like this and want to find out more about me check out my blog (http://dreamtime.logic11.com). I post almost every day, and a lot of things I post are fiction, some of which I don't publish anywhere else.

If you want to support me, you can also support me on Patreon (https://www.patreon.com/logic11).

This is book one in a series, but the rest of the series starts twenty years in the future. Keep an eye out.

Get the sequel for free!

It's been twenty years since the dead rose to consume the living, and humanity has survived, at least in one small corner of the world. The city of New Hope is growing and running out of space so they send a force out to take back a nearby island from the hordes of zombies that shamble through its streets.

The island is home to another group of survivors though, a cannibal cult that worships the undead and doesn't want to share.

Chad is young, newly trained, he finds himself in the midst of hordes of zombies as the only member of his squad not captured by the cannibal cult. It is up to him to save the rest.

Tamra is an actress on the only TV station left on earth, but she wants to be more, she wants to be a real hero. She throws herself into the middle of the mission, heedless of her own safety. Skills she developed in the early days of the post-apocalyptic period.

Tyson worked construction, trying to reclaim resources from the ruined world. The cult captures him and now he must struggle every moment to survive and to maintain his sanity.

All of these disparate characters are desperate to return to their home, to survive, to defeat religious fanatics and thousands of undead who still wander the world.

You can get Resource Economies (book 2 of the world of the dead series) for free! Just subscribe to my mailing list [1]at http://bit.ly/2K99oBP-resource-economies-free-ebook and I will send it to you. I use my list to keep my readers up to date on what I'm doing and what I'm writing. I will never sell or give away your information.

---

1.   http://bit.ly/2K99oBP-resource-economies-free-ebook

Don't miss out!

Visit the website below and you can sign up to receive emails whenever Traverse Davies publishes a new book. There's no charge and no obligation.

https://books2read.com/r/B-A-KAEI-HGUY

BOOKS 2 READ

Connecting independent readers to independent writers.

Also by Traverse Davies

World of the Dead
A Long Walk
Resource Economies: Reclaiming the Zombie Apocalypse

Watch for more at https://dreamtime.logic11.com.

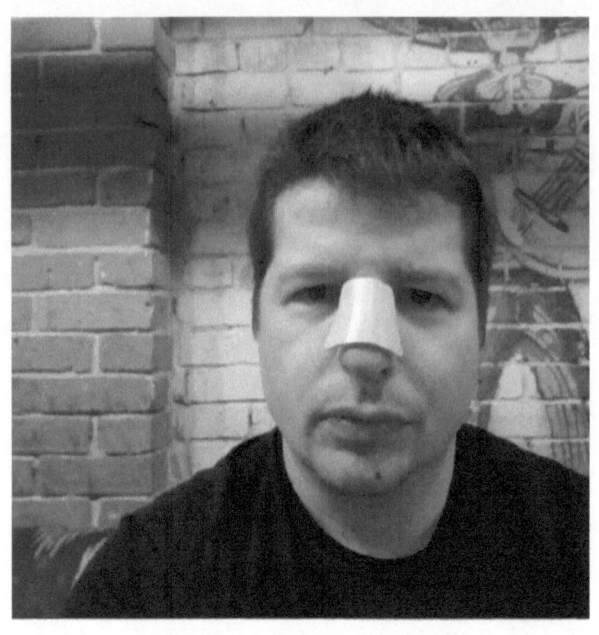

About the Author

Traverse Davies was raised by a pack of wild hippies, during the seventies and eighties when such creatures roamed the forests unfettered and free. He discovered a love of books at an early age, and that love has only grown over the years. After years of working in IT he decided to branch out in the activities he did while hunched in front of a glowing screen tapping at a keyboard and added writing to his task list. His skills outside of programming and writing include Taekwondo, Wilderness Survival (sort of), Ninjutsu, Parkour, Drawing, Photography, and crappy Photoshop work. He has lived in various countries, although he currently resides on the east coast of Canada. He is obsessed with post-apocalyptic survival and subverting as many genre's as possible

Read more at https://dreamtime.logic11.com.